# CROSS-FIRE

*A Vietnam Novel*

# CROSS-FIRE

*A Vietnam Novel*

———

BY GAIL GRAHAM

ILLUSTRATIONS BY DAVID STONE MARTIN

Pantheon Books

*C, 1*

LIBRARY OF CONGRESS CATALOGING IN PUBLICATION DATA
Graham, Gail B
  Cross-fire.
  SUMMARY: A soldier lost from his platoon finds four enemy
children, the only survivors of a village raid, and together they begin
a hopeless struggle for survival in the Vietnamese jungle.
  [1. Vietnamese Conflict, 1961–    —Fiction]
I. Title.
PZ7.G75168Cr        [Fic]        71-175953
ISBN 0-394-82380-X
ISBN 0-394-92380-4 (lib. bdg.)
          *Manufactured in the United States of America*

—BL   NOV 13

To Mother and Harry
with love

# CROSS-FIRE

*A Vietnam Novel*

An American private separated from his unit finds four Vietnamese children. Though enemies, they struggle together to survive.

# ONE

He lay very still, face down and breathless, his face pressed close against the swampy earth. He was alive. The ground was soft and uneven; now he could feel that his left foot lay in a puddle full of water. It had soaked through his pants and his socks.

The clamminess and the smell of mud and rotting vegetation told him that he was still alive. He opened his eyes, and turned his head very carefully, waiting for pain that did not come. He moved his arms. His arms were all right. Slowly, carefully, he sat up. There was still no pain.

"Hey." His voice was cracked and strange in the silence.

He peered about. He was in a muddy clearing, surrounded on all sides by the hunched and twisted greenery of this God-forsaken, nightmare jungle. You could buy jackets in Saigon that said: *When I die I'll go to heaven 'cause I've served my time in hell.* That was the truth.

"Hey," he said, more loudly. "Hey! Can anybody hear me? Conn? Rick?"

The silence made him uneasy. It wasn't natural. The sun beat down upon the mud and the green slime, so bright it made your eyes hurt. The sky was a funny gray color, sitting low over the country like an invisible, suffocating blanket. He was perspiring and he was having trouble breathing . . . he hadn't been able to breathe right ever since he'd left the staging area in Quan Long.

They wouldn't all go off and leave him here. He wasn't dead. Hell, he wasn't even hurt. It was some kind of a trap. His M-16 lay where it had fallen, a few feet away from him. He reached for it, and cradled it in his arms. It was some kind of a trap.

"Okay, Charlie. I know you're out there. You might as well come on out."

He clicked the safety back, ready.

The silence was like a ringing in his ears, an ache that he couldn't quite define. It roared in soundless, invisible circles, tightening about his chest so that he was conscious of the effort it took just to breathe. It wasn't natural that a place should be so quiet . . . there weren't any quiet places in Vietnam.

He swallowed painfully. It was like before the homecoming game. He could hear his heart beating. But this wasn't any game.

The rest of the patrol was dead. Face it man, they're dead. Dave and Billy Lee and Rick and Conn, they were dead. If they were alive, they wouldn't have gone off and left him lying in the mud.

And Charlie was waiting in the bushes beyond the clearing—waiting and watching to see what the round-eyes was going to do.

He plucked a grenade from his belt and hefted it in his left hand. He looked at it. Puckered greenish gray . . . some of the guys called them pineapples. They *looked* like pineapples, little dried-up pineapples.

Pull the pin and you've got five seconds.

He wondered what time it was. The sun was hidden behind the opaque cloud-cover, and he looked at his watch. The crystal was smashed; the hands and luminous dial were smeared with reddish-colored mud already drying into clay. He wiped it clean, but it was no good. He didn't know what time it was—he didn't even know what time it had been when the watch had stopped. It must have been toward dawn, the dark, cold time just before the sky lightened and the sun came up.

The reconnaissance patrol had left Hung My last night just after dark, headed south for a link-up with another patrol that was coming north out of Cai Nuoc. They'd sweated their way through the mud and the moonless night of the monsoon forest, looking for Charlie. It wasn't a very big patrol. There were just five of them, and the lieutenant. Something big was in the air, but the non-coms didn't know what it was and they weren't supposed to know.

They'd been out for nearly eight hours when the first sniper opened fire. No sweat. They trained you for six weeks at Schofield in Hawaii, and as he and Conn had moved together through the meshed vines and the mud, shoulders hunched and bayonets ready, he'd felt good, like something was finally coming true.

They'd stumbled onto something. God knows what. The sniper fire was scattered and spread out. You knew there were at least three of them, maybe more.

Someone yelled. The firing stopped, and then started up again. He and Conn separated. He'd kept his head down, moving slowly and watching where he stepped. He'd seen a Joe in Saigon sitting in a wheelchair and waiting to go back to the States. He didn't have any legs. Nothing like that was going to happen to him. It happened to other guys, but it wasn't going to happen to him. It'd be better to die, than to live like that.

So he'd been moving slowly toward where most of the shooting seemed to be coming from, listening and watching and ready. He remembered the clearing. He'd hung back, afraid of the open space and the easy going. And then . . . he didn't remember. It seemed to him that someone lobbed in a grenade, but he didn't remember.

He didn't know what had happened, but he knew that he was alive. And that was something. For now, it was enough.

Slowly, he got to his feet. His head hurt, but it wasn't enough to bother him. He thought he smelled something . . . smoke. He sniffed. He wasn't sure. He double-checked the M-16 and moved forward toward the center of the clearing, cradling the M-16 close to his body and still holding onto the grenade.

C'mon, Charlie. Here I am. Come and get me, Charlie. C'mon, Charlie. I'm right here waiting for you, even got a little present for you. C'mon . . .

The fat, green leaves and vines that shrouded the clearing were motionless beneath the sun's diffused glare. There was no sound. There was no movement. There was nothing . . . nothing. He hesitated. He didn't know what to do.

Stupid to carry the grenade around. He'd need both

6

hands to pull the pin, and he wasn't going to drop the M-16 to do it. He put it back on his belt.

All this time, all through the slow, silent minutes, something like sickness had been coiled inside of him, coiled tight and ugly like the leeches and the awful crawling things they taught you about at Schofield. Now it stirred, moving through his body, through his arms and legs and into his fingertips. It made him want to scream, to run. He fought it.

C'mon, Charlie. C'mon . . .

It takes a smart man to know enough to be afraid, Dad had said during that last weekend leave. And don't let any of 'em tell you different.

He didn't remember much about that weekend. Funny, you'd think a guy'd remember every little detail of something like that, but he didn't. He didn't even remember what he'd been wearing. It was all mixed together, it was like people acting in a play where nobody really believes what's happening. He'd kissed Mom and he'd shaken hands with Dad, but he hadn't felt any different than he'd felt the other times he'd said good-bye to them—fishing trips, backpacking in the Sierras, two weeks in New York City visiting with Uncle Martin, things like that. But Mom had started to cry, and he didn't know what to do or what to say to her. He remembered that she'd been wearing a pink apron, a pink apron with white lace around the edges of it, and that he'd been embarrassed when she'd started to cry.

He'd promised her that he'd write every week, but he didn't. With all the things they found for you to do, he didn't have as much time for writing letters as he'd thought he would. And he had to be real careful of what he wrote and how he spelled things. One of the guys in his outfit wrote a letter to his family, and his mom went and sent it to the local newspaper and they printed it just like it was, with a dozen words spelled wrong. He grinned, remembering. His own mother wrote every week. Nice, long letters.

He wasn't afraid now. He stood up a little straighter, and loosened his grip on the M-16. There wasn't anybody here. There wasn't anybody at all.

Behind him, a bird called out once and was silent. It didn't sound like a signal. It just sounded like a bird.

It was then that he saw the dark place in the grass, ahead of him and just a little bit to his left. It looked like it might be mud, but it was the wrong color. He knelt down and touched it, but even before his fingers came away sticky with the stuff, he knew it was blood, human blood drying slowly on the marshy grass.

His stomach clenched and he twisted away, doubling up. The sickness passed as quickly as it had come. He shivered, and there was a cold sweat on his forehead and on the palms of his hands.

He took deep breaths, knowing that he had to either pull himself together or die in the jungle.

He wondered if the other guys got as scared as this. It wasn't the kind of thing you talked about. You didn't even kid about it. It was like death. Nobody talked about death, either.

Okay. He was okay now. He put the blood out of his mind as if it hadn't happened or he hadn't seen it, and he was okay.

The bushes rustled in front of him, and he froze. The rustling stopped. Crouching, he peered into the dark green murk of vines and low-lying shrubs, trying to pinpoint the place where the bushes had rustled. It was very still. He took the grenade from his belt and cupped it in

8

the palm of his hand. He looked at the pin. He'd pull the pin and heave it into the bushes, just to be on the safe side.

The heavy, hot silence of the clearing throbbed in his head like a pain. If he threw the grenade at nothing, it would be as good as telling Charlie where he was. He stood motionless, listening and watching.

Somebody was watching him. He could feel it, he could feel that he was being watched. Get it over with, one way or the other. Bayonet mounted and ready, he clipped the grenade back onto his belt and moved slowly forward toward the place where the bushes had rustled.

A step. Another step. And then he saw the two black, shiny eyes peering out at him. Lunging forward, he thrust to kill, the bayonet's tip poised to sink itself into the steady, unblinking eyes.

A scream split the air and a clawing, yelling thing with flying hair catapulted at him from the left, butting him hard just below the left kidney and dragging him down sideways into the muck. The M-16 flew out of his hands, but even as he fell, he drew his knife for close-in fighting. This was it, baby. This was it.

He jerked his left elbow back, catching his assailant in the gut and breaking free. This one was small and skinny, even for a Vietnamese, and collapsed beneath his down-chopped fist like something made of twigs and paper. He straddled the crumpled body, knife ready.

And then he stopped cold, staring. It was a girl.

She opened her eyes and stared up at him with a look that made him think of the bobcat they'd once trapped in the San Bernardino Mountains. She wasn't much of a girl, not anywhere near five feet tall, and starved-looking in the shapeless, black pajamas she wore. Not even twelve years old, he guessed. A kid.

"Don't move," he warned her.

She stared up at him, motionless and uncomprehending. She probably thought he was going to kill her. Maybe he'd have to. He grabbed for the M-16, got it, and aimed. She still hadn't moved.

"Do you speak English? Do you understand English?"

Fear glittered in her eyes. Slowly, she moved her head from side to side.

Conscious of his size and of the M-16, he moved a step or so away from her. She could sit up if she wanted to. But she lay there in the mud, following every move he made with her bright, fear-stricken eyes.

"Did I hurt you? Are you hurt?"

She didn't move.

"Why'd you do that? Why'd you try to jump me like that?"

It wasn't any good. She didn't speak any English, and anybody could see she was scared half to death.

He looked at her, scowling, and then he jerked his head in the direction of the bushes. "Who's that in there? Who's hiding there?"

She started to scramble to her feet, moving quickly and gracefully like a cat, but he waved the M-16 at her and she sank back, squatting on her haunches in the mud. "Don't you move. Just you sit right there and tell me who you've got hiding in those bushes. Charlie? V.C.? Huh?"

She said something, in Vietnamese.

"No Charlie?"

More Vietnamese. Sing-song gibberish that meant nothing.

"I don't understand you. I don't understand a word you say. Listen, don't you speak *any* English?" She stared, uncomprehending.

"Okay, listen. You go and show me."

The girl looked at him, wide-eyed and silent. She was kind of a pretty girl, or she would be when she grew up. Now she was just a flat-chested kid, but her hair was long and shiny and her eyes were something else. Her feet were bare and dirty, and there was dirt smeared on her arms and face from rolling around in the mud. But she was pretty, all the same. He guessed that it was her eyes that made her pretty.

He gestured toward the jungle. "Go and show me what's out there. But don't try any funny stuff, you hear me?" He hefted the M-16 as menacingly as he could, and she shrank back. "Go on." And he waved her toward the bushes.

She didn't move.

He stood up. Grabbing her about one wrist, he hauled her to her feet and shoved her gently in the direction of the bushes. "Go on. I want to see what's hiding in those bushes."

She went slowly, looking fearfully back at him with every step she took. He didn't know whether he ought to shoot her or not. It wouldn't be the first time Charlie used a girl for a decoy. It might be that the whole thing was a booby trap, that Charlie was in back of him and all around him and any minute a bunch of yelling, screaming little yellow men with bare feet and scrounged guns . . .

She'd reached the edge of the clearing now. She gave him one last look, knelt, and seemed to pick something up. He couldn't see what it was. She shielded it with her body. It looked like a bundle of rags. Then it moved, and he saw that it had arms and legs. "Hey, it's a baby. That isn't *your* baby, is it?"

She stood before him, holding the baby close against

her and staring at him out of big, almond-shaped eyes that told him nothing. The M-16 felt heavy in his arms. He'd never heard of Charlie using a little baby for a decoy, he'd never heard of anything like that. Not even at Schofield. He shifted his weight from one foot to the other. He didn't know what the hell to do.

"Is that your baby? Are you the baby's mother? Are you mama-san?" he asked, like some of the airmen he knew who'd been stationed in Tokyo and spoke to the Vietnamese as they'd spoken to the Japanese, calling them mama-san or papa-san.

She shook her head.

"No mama-san?"

He moved toward her and she backed away from him, away from the gleaming tip of the bayonet. She stumbled, and clutched the baby closer to her flat chest. He stood still, embarrassed. "Listen, I won't hurt you, if you're on the level. We don't go around killing kids, for God's sake."

She stared at him, silent, holding the baby.

"Hey. How come that baby doesn't make any noise? Is he sick?"

She didn't understand; he knew that she didn't understand a single word of what he'd been saying, except maybe that bit about mama-san.

A stepped-on twig snapped sharp and crisp as a sniper's bullet, and he whirled toward the sound of it, pressing the trigger of the M-16 as easily and as naturally as breathing, and emptying the magazine into the impenetrable brush blindly, not realizing what he was doing until the sound of the bullets reverberated in his ears.

The girl screamed.

"No Charlie, huh?" he snarled at her, hating her

feigned innocence and despising his own innocence at having been taken in by her. "Was that Charlie? Huh? Was it?"

Her face was blank with horror. She ignored him, half-turning toward the place where the bullets had shredded through the thick weave of vine and vegetation and calling out in words he didn't know, the same words over and over again. Ton, it sounded like. Ton. Ton. Over and over again.

"Shut up!" But she wasn't paying any attention to him now. Like he didn't even exist.

"Listen! You cut that out or . . ."

A voice, high and thin like hers, called back from someplace beyond the tangle of leaves. His heart thudding, he stepped in front of the girl and pressed the muzzle of the M-16 against the baby's head. The girl froze.

"You tell him to come out of there with his hands up, or the kid's dead and so are you."

She did not move. She did not even seem to be breathing.

He knew that he ought to shoot. You don't take prisoners in the jungle. So he'd kill them both, and he'd kill their buddy in the bushes, and then he'd get the hell out of here the best way he could.

Behind him, the grass rustled. He turned, but he wasn't fast enough. There were two children standing at the edge of the clearing, a boy and a girl. They were small and barefoot and ragged. They stood with their arms hanging loosely at their sides. Their eyes were wide, and looking past him at the girl.

Taken aback, he lowered the M-16. The girl said something, and the two children sidled past him to stand beside her. The little girl reached out and clutched the edge of the older one's pajamas. The little one looked as if she was maybe three years old, and the boy certainly wasn't much older.

All three of them stared at him, waiting. He guessed that they were related—brother and sisters, maybe. Beautiful. What the hell was he supposed to do now?

A heavy, pelting rain began to pour down upon them from the lowering sky. The drops came thick and fast, so big that they hurt and so many of them that they made a curtain of gray, shutting out the lines of the jungle.

The girl pulled an edge of a tattered rag over the baby's head. The other children were drenched in moments, their black hair pasted to their skulls like a glossy cap. Water streamed down their faces like tears.

"Do you live around here?" he asked. "Do you know someplace where we can get out of the rain? Shelter?"

Useless. Might just as well talk to a bunch of statues.

The rain poured down. It was as if someone had upended a bucket of warm, gray water. He'd never seen rain like the rain they had in this country. It rained in California; every winter it rained like crazy for a couple of weeks, and then that was all the rain there'd be until the next winter. But this rain came sneaky and sudden—one minute you were in a field, the next minute it was a swamp. Guys got drowned on patrol in flash floods. You heard stories about it.

The girl and the children hadn't moved. They wouldn't move until he did. They were scared to death.

He'd learned how to make a shelter while he was in training at Schofield. They'd spent a whole week learning to weave the flat, slick leaves into a sort of roof . . . there was no sense in standing here, getting soaked. And the rain could last for hours.

"Come on," he said.

He walked to the edge of the clearing. They didn't budge. Like statues, he thought again. He wondered what they were thinking. He couldn't see their eyes through the curtain of rain. He hesitated, and then shrugged. They were three little kids and a baby, and he still had plenty of ammo and his grenades. They couldn't hurt him.

There was a chance that they were working for Charlie. There was that chance.

But he couldn't shoot down three kids.

Once and for all, he turned his back on them and plunged into the twining, overgrown jungle beyond the clearing.

# TWO

In the morning, Mi had heard the drone of the American aircraft. She'd peered up at the sky, but the planes were flying so fast and so high that none of the women —not even sharp-eyed old Grandmother Nam—could boast that she'd actually seen one of them. The Americans had been flying over the village every morning and every evening for the past month. No one knew why. They'd done no harm, but everyone had heard stories of what happened in other villages once the Americans started sending planes over them, and people were uneasy.

"They are going north," Hung Ba told the women. "See how high they are! They're not interested in us. And why should they be? We've nothing here but rice and babies and women, and one old man."

Hung Ba had already been an old man during the war with the French. Nobody knew how old Hung Ba really was; Mi didn't even think that Hung Ba knew anymore. Hung Ba could read from the newspapers that occasionally made their way to the village, and he claimed that he could speak French. It was whispered that Hung Ba had fought with the Viet Minh and that even now . . . but it was better not to speak of such things.

Despite Hung Ba's reassurances that the planes were too high to harm them, the women and girls were anxious. Whenever the planes flew over the village, they stopped gossiping, stopped cooking, stopped whatever they were doing and watched, eyes skyward, until the planes were gone. Even the children were quiet at such times.

"It's a shame to frighten the children," Hung Ba would say angrily.

But one could not help what one felt.

Other than Hung Ba, there were no men in the village. All of them had gone to fight in the Army or—if they were fortunate enough to be too old for the Army or to have enough money to bribe the officials in Saigon —to work on the American bases. The Americans were said to be loud and barbarous and even unintelligent, but there was one thing that everyone agreed upon: the Americans were foolish with their money, even more foolish than the French had been. If a man could only manage to work for the Americans, then that man would surely become rich.

As always, the rich men in Saigon gathered in the biggest share of American dollars; it had always been thus in Vietnam. But after the highly-born and the highly-placed had taken their lion's share of the dollars, even the poorest peasant fresh from the village—if he was clever and thrifty and knew a few English words—could make his fortune. Mi's father worked for the Americans at the huge Bien Hoa base, driving a truck back and forth between Bien Hoa and Saigon. He'd been gone for nearly a year, but he'd come home twice, bringing canned foods and plastic shoes for Bong and the baby and once, a radio.

With the men gone, the village seemed shrunken and unreal. One got so tired of living with women and children! Mi would be so glad when the war was done, and the young men came back . . . she blushed and giggled at the unmaidenly boldness of such thoughts.

In other times, Mi would have been betrothed by now; perhaps she would have been married, and carrying a baby in her belly like Bich Ti. Of course, no one knew where Bich Ti's husband was now, whether he was alive or dead. It was better to be unmarried, Mi decided, than to be married and with child and without a husband at your side.

"Mi! What are you doing with those clothes—washing them or pickling them?"

Mi started, and smiled. Working quickly, she wrung out the last of the clothes that she was supposed to have been rinsing, and hung them onto a bare-twigged bush to dry. "I'll go and get Ton," she said.

"He'll be hungry. You'd think that his stomach would tell him when it's time to eat." Mama smiled, and poked the coals in the brazier into flame. "A full-grown man couldn't do a better job than Ton has done," she boasted.

Nine years old and small for his age, Ton had been working full twelve-hour days in the rice paddies ever since Papa had gone to Bien Hoa. Everyone was proud of him—other women prodded their own sons and held Ton up as an example of what a good son ought to be.

Humming softly, Mi strolled down the beaten path between the village's dozen huts. Bong and the baby were playing in the dust.

"Come walk with me to the paddies!" Mi called to them.

Bong scrambled to her feet and set the baby onto her hip, just as Mi used to carry Ton upon *her* hip when she was no older than Bong was now. The sisters walked side by side through the tall grasses and the cool mud, Bong taking two hurrying steps for every one of Mi's. The baby cooed and gurgled and snatched at the folds of Mi's pajamas. So peaceful, Mi thought. She was glad that the planes were gone.

Bong was chattering on about what the baby's name ought to be. It was a family joke, Bong and the baby. Bong was so absorbed with her tiny brother that the rest of them called her "Littlest Mother."

They were perhaps a kilometer from the village when it happened. Suddenly, there were three gray planes high over the village. They circled, then dipped, lower and lower in the sky until Mi could see quite clearly that they were Americans . . . and then, dozens of oblong, gray objects rained from the underbellies of the three swooping planes, falling slowly and silently, so that they seemed to be floating in the air . . .

Dragging the two children along with her, Mi flung herself to the ground.

For a long moment, all was still. Then the earth buckled beneath them like an angry dragon, and Bong screamed for Mama and the baby began to cry and Mi shut her eyes and thought, this is what it is to die.

Something else . . . an odor, a smell of burning. The earth shuddered, and lay still. Mi raised her head, but she could see nothing save billow upon billow of inky black smoke, blotting out everything. The jungle, the sky, the vanishing American planes—all were hidden by the blackness that was everywhere. Like sorcery, a huge and towering column of orange flame licked suddenly skyward only a hundred meters from where they lay, and Mi drew Bong and the baby close against her, trying to shield them.

Far away, people were screaming.

It could not possibly be real. It could not possibly be happening. If I'm dreaming, Mi thought, let me wake up, please let me wake up . . .

Minutes passed. How many minutes? Mi didn't know. She did not move; she *could* not move. Her body seemed shackled to the damp, dark earth.

The screams stopped.

Slowly, she sat up. She heard the sullen, crackling sound of fire, the occasional hiss as flame met water at the edge of the marsh.

She ought to do something. She ought to run back to the village, to try to help . . .

Hung Ba had known this would happen. Trying to convince the other men that it was wrong to seek work on the American bases, Hung Ba had shown them pictures of villages burned and charred into nothingness. Like little fish that have fallen into a cooking-fire, Hung Ba told them.

But the men had gone, despite Hung Ba. There was money to be made. And a man had to think of his family.

Hung Ba was right, thought Mi. And now our village is like the villages in those pictures. And the people . . .

Grandmother Nam and Bich Ti and Mrs. Thuy and Mama and even Hung Ba himself . . . now, they are like little fish, too. Little fish that have fallen into a cooking-fire.

But perhaps someone is still alive, Mi thought then. Alive and hurt and needing help—needing *my* help.

Bong began to cry.

Mi picked up the baby and held it close to her. I must go back to the village, she told herself. I must make sure . . .

"I want Mama!" sobbed Bong. "I want Mama!"

"Not now, Bong. Not—not now."

Bong huddled against Mi, and stared fearfully up at the smoke-smudged sky.

"Mi?" Bong's voice was very small and very frightened.

"What is it, little sister?"

"Ton . . . where is Ton?"

Ton! She'd forgotten about Ton. Instinctively, Mi looked out across the swamp, toward the rice paddies. So far as she could see, the fires had not come beyond the edge of the marsh. Ton might still be alive, hiding as they were hiding . . . but alive!

She stood up, still holding the baby.

The fire had already burned itself out. In the distance, Mi thought she heard the faraway drone of an airplane. She looked up, searching the sky. But there was nothing . . . nothing at all except for a few last wisps of blackish-gray smoke.

She must go back to the village. And she must find Ton—if he was still alive.

"Where are you going?" asked Bong.

She hesitated. "I'm—I'm going to find Ton."

Bong scrambled to her feet and clutched at Mi's hand.

"I want to go, too."

"No. You've got to stay here and take care of the baby."

"I don't want to. I'm afraid."

"There's nothing to be afraid of. Nothing," repeated Mi, firmly. "Do you think that I'd go away and leave you, if I thought that anything bad would happen?"

Bong thought about that for a moment. "And when you come back, will we go home?"

Home, thought Mi. If only there was someplace that they could call home!

"We'll see," she told Bong. "Here, sit down and I'll put the baby in your lap. That's right. Now, I want you to stay right here. Don't even get up, until I come back. Do you understand?"

Bong nodded.

Leaving them there, Mi made her way through the marsh to where the rice paddies lay. The place seemed to be deserted.

"Ton!" she called uneasily. "Ton, are you here?"

The paddies themselves looked just as they always looked; neat squares of calm water separated one from the next by little dikes of carefully-mounded earth. Just at the surface of the water, row upon row of tiny green shoots peeped up.

Mi turned away quickly. Perhaps Ton was dead, after all. Perhaps he'd gone back to the village. Perhaps he'd taken the short-cut through the wallow . . .

There was only one way to find out.

But Mi didn't move. She didn't want to go back to the village. She didn't want to see what had happened. She was afraid . . .

Yet she knew that she must go back.

She forced herself to walk slowly along the marsh path

that bypassed the wallow. Her legs felt weak and rubbery, and her knees were shaking so badly that she could scarcely keep her balance as she crossed the single bamboo pole that served as a bridge over the wettest, muddiest part of the wallow. A few steps farther, and a strange, acrid odor filled the still-smoky air. It was the odor of burned flesh. Mi stumbled, and leaned against the trunk of a tree and closed her eyes. She could not go on. She could not go into the village. She simply could not.

She stood there for several minutes, unable to force herself forward and yet unwilling to go back without finding out what had happened to Ton. It was very, very still. Mi held her breath and listened for the sound of the baby's crying, but even that had ceased.

It was only a little farther. She was only a dozen steps from the clump of banana trees that shielded the western end of the village from the monsoon winds. She would go now—she would go quickly, so that it would soon be finished.

Almost running, she pushed through the rows of banana trees, shoving the stalks of half-grown fruit out of her way as she went.

And here was the village.

It was not what she had expected. It was not like Hung Ba's pictures. It was simply . . . no more. It was hard to believe that less than an hour ago, this had been a village. The earth was charred an ugly black, and everything was gone—the huts, the carts, the nets, the hammocks, the people—gone as if they had never existed.

Numb with disbelief, Mi took a step forward. Another step. The ground was still warm; she could feel the warmth through the soles of her sandals. Another step. A stick thrust up out of the ground, black and smoldering. It was all that was left of the end-pole of one of the huts. Mi reached out and touched it, and it collapsed into a heap of embers and ashes at her feet.

The terrible smell of burning flesh was everywhere, and Mi held her breath against it. Here and there on the flat, parched char lay little black mounds . . . bodies, Mi thought, and her stomach churned.

She couldn't stand anymore, and she turned and ran back through the clump of banana trees, toward the wallow. Everyone was dead, and Ton was dead too. Her legs crumpled beneath her and she fell to her knees in the mud, sobbing helplessly.

"Mi! Mi! Is that you?"

Startled, she sprang to her feet.

"You're alive!"

"And *you* . . ." began Mi, but she couldn't go on.

Ton looked dazed. "But—but how?"

"We'd just left the village, just before it happened," explained Mi. "Bong and the baby and me. We were coming to tell you that it was time to come home."

"Then they're alive too!"

Mi nodded.

"But where are they? Why aren't they with you? Were they hurt? Were they burned?"

"No. I left them over there, on the other side of the marsh. I didn't know—I didn't know if you were alive or not. And I didn't know . . . I thought maybe there might be somebody left alive, but I thought it would be better to leave Bong where she was," Mi finished shakily. She looked at Ton. "Have you been . . . have you seen it? The village?"

He nodded.

Ton looked away—up at the empty sky—and his face

was terrible. "Someday I'll kill them. I will. I'll kill them."

A man could not cry. A man had to vent his sorrow in words and deeds, rather than in tears. Today, Ton had become a man. Mi's heart ached for him. She reached out and touched his arm, very gently.

"I know," she said. "But we've got to think about what we're going to do."

He looked at her, surprised. "Do? What is there to do now? Everyone's dead."

"We're not dead. You and I and Bong and the baby— we four are alive. And well. And we've got to stay that way, don't you see? We'll need food, and shelter. Milk for the baby, if we can get it. And we can't stay here. It's not safe, not now. We've got to think about where we're going to go."

"To Saigon," said Ton flatly, as if it had already been decided. "To Papa. Where else?"

Saigon, thought Mi. Hundreds of miles walking to the north over washed-out roads and through burned-out villages. Without money. Without food. With only the clothes that they wore. And even if they managed to do it, it would be difficult to find Papa there. Maybe impossible. The city was swollen with refugees (Papa himself had said so), all of them penniless, hungry, searching . . .

"You've said it yourself. We can't stay here. And besides, Papa will think we're dead."

He was right. It would have to be Saigon.

They stood there a moment longer, side by side, looking back toward the place that had been their home. They stood there saying good-bye.

"Come on, then. Let's go and get the children."

They went, slowly.

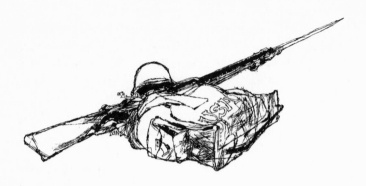

# THREE

They squatted there, the three of them (the oldest, the girl with the doe-eyes, was holding the baby), watching every move he made. It'd taken him nearly ten minutes to persuade them to come in out of the rain. Harry shook his head. He'd never seen kids that acted like these. There must be something wrong with them, he thought, shell shock maybe, or maybe they were sick.

The rain pattered down, not loud, but drowning out everything else. It made a funny, clattering sound on the leaves of the shelter above their heads.

"Well, where do we go from here?" Harry asked them. But they just looked at him.

"Listen, you don't have to be afraid of me. I'm not going to hurt you."

Man, he wished they'd stop looking at him like that.

You'd think they were about to be murdered, the way they were looking at him. Crazy, dumb kids. A man doesn't go and build a lean-to for a bunch of kids that he's planning to kill, couldn't they at least figure that out?

"And you don't speak any English, do you?" Harry said to the girl. "Not even a couple of words."

Of course they didn't.

And then he remembered about the book, that little book that he'd stuck into his hip pocket a couple of days ago and . . . yeah. It was still there. He pulled it out and held it up triumphantly. The girl leaned forward a little, trying to see the picture on the cover. It was a picture of a Vietnamese girl in a white and yellow flowered *ao dai,* riding a bicycle past a bunch of white geese. Kind of corny, Harry thought.

"It's a book about Vietnam. The army hands them out to us, so we can read up on what the country's like and not go around insulting people by mistake, see?"

He held it out to her. She hesitated.

"Go ahead. Take a look at it. It won't bite you."

She handed the baby to the boy and then she reached out her hand and took it, carefully, almost as if she expected it to blow up in her face.

"You're supposed to open it. Turn the pages."

She didn't move.

Maybe she'd never seen a book before. This was pretty far out in the country, and most of the people were as poor as mud hens. Ignorant, too. No schools or anything like that. Like savages, almost.

"It's a sort of guidebook," Harry said. He knew that she didn't understand him, but it made him feel better to talk, to hear the sound of his own voice. "It's got all kinds of different things in it, pictures and stuff like that. Lots of pictures. Here, why don't you let me show you?" He reached out and took the booklet from her unresisting fingers.

They all sat back then, watching him as he turned the pages. They didn't look quite as scared as they'd looked a couple of minutes ago. The baby woke up, looked at him and then went back to sleep. It was a quiet baby. Cute, too.

Hey, here was something that she'd understand. People celebrating the Vietnamese New Year, beating on gongs and eating little cakes.

"*Tet*," said Harry, showing her the pictures. "*Tet Nguyen Dan,* right?"

She smiled. "*Tet*," she repeated.

The little girl said something then, and giggled and clapped her hand over her mouth.

"What's the matter? Didn't I say it right?"

He gave her what he thought was a reassuring smile, but she just moved as far away from him as she could, as if she thought she'd done something wrong and was going to be punished for it. If only there was some way to get through to them, Harry thought, to make them understand that he wanted to be their friend, that he wasn't going to hurt them. They'd probably never seen an American soldier before. Maybe it was the uniform that was scaring them.

The eldest girl was leafing through the army booklet, looking at the pictures. Watching her, Harry wondered how old she was. You just couldn't tell with Vietnamese women. He'd seen grandmothers who looked like teenagers, graceful and slim and not a line on their faces. A few of the guys thought that they were really something else, Vietnamese girls, but Harry didn't think they were all that wonderful. Most of them were too skinny, like this one. Look at her arms, look at her neck, you could almost count the bones. Too skinny. Still, she was pretty in a kind of pathetic way, appealing, like a puppy or a stray kitten.

She looked up at him then, all excited, and tried to show him something in the booklet. Leaning forward, Harry looked at what had caught her eye. *Useful Phrases.*

Yeah! He'd forgotten all about it. Toward the back of the booklet there was a whole section on the Vietnamese language, with sentences and conversations and everything. Harry had never been much for learning foreign languages—he'd had a little bit of Spanish in high school, and that had been enough for him—but a few of the guys in his outfit knew how to say simple things like "hello" and "thank you" and "how much?" and it was really something to see, the way they could bargain on a street corner for a pack of gum or a carton of black-market cigarettes. And there was one guy—Nate Daniels —who spent all his spare time in the sack, studying Vietnamese out of a real textbook. Nate, he could jabber away like a native. Too bad *he* wasn't here.

He glanced down the list of Useful Phrases, looking for something easy to start with. Hello, goodbye, good morning, good afternoon, good night—it was all the same word. *Chao ong.*

"*Chao ong,*" Harry said.

Both girls giggled.

Harry didn't care. He'd rather have them laughing— even if they were laughing at him—than sitting there and waiting for him to shoot them.

"Okay, let me try it again. *Chao ong.*"

The eldest girl smiled. "*Chao ong.*"

"It sure sounds different when you say it. *Chao ong.* How was that?"

She nodded, and said something in Vietnamese.

"I'll be right with you," Harry told her. "All these little doodles over the words, what do they mean? It ought to be in here somewhere." He thumbed rapidly back toward the beginning of the language section. "Let me just see if I can dope this out, okay?"

It was getting dark, and the rain didn't help much. He had to hold the booklet up close to his face in order to see the words. "Yeah, here it is. 'There is considerable difference between the way Vietnamese is spoken in various parts of the country,' " he read aloud. " 'If you learn the southern accent, you may be able to understand people from the north but not necessarily those from central Vietnam. Vietnamese in the central provinces of Thanh Hoa and'—sorry, I can't pronounce this next one—'have an accent that even their fellow countrymen from other districts find difficult to understand.' "

Harry looked up. "Doesn't help much, does it?"

There were three or four complicated-looking paragraphs that explained how the different letters were pronounced, but skimming over them, Harry couldn't figure out what they were talking about. It was a lot harder than he thought it would be, Vietnamese. And in a little while, it would be too dark to see anything at all. Might as well go ahead and take a crack at it, Harry decided, and even if they could only understand half of what he said, at least they'd be able to communicate. You couldn't get very far on *chao ong*.

He turned back to the Useful Phrases. "The way I figure it, the first thing we ought to do is to get introduced. Now, my name is Harry. What's your name?" He ran his forefinger down the columns, looking for the Vietnamese phrase for "What is your name?"

It wasn't there.

Damn! If that wasn't just like the U.S. Army. They gave you every kind of information except what you needed, and they expected you to go out and win a war. Right in front of the book, they knock themselves out to tell you how polite and cultured the Vietnamese people are . . . and then they don't even bother telling you how to find out a person's name. Jesus Christ almighty! He closed the book.

"Okay, gang. Here we go. Harry," he said, and tapped his chest. "Harry. My name is Harry. Get it?"

They looked puzzled.

"Harry. I am Harry."

The little girl laughed, and tapped her own chest, imitating him. "Haa-lee," she said. "Haa-lee."

"No, no, you're not Harry. *I'm* Harry."

She thought he was playing some kind of game. He turned to the eldest girl. "Look. Pay attention. I'm Harry. My name is Harry." He tapped his chest again. "Harry."

"Haa-lee," she replied, softly.

But he could tell that she didn't understand, that she was just trying to be polite or to humor him or something. He'd have to try something else. But what? How do you talk to people who don't speak English?

"Wait a minute," Harry said. "Just wait a minute. I think I've got it." Reaching into his back pocket, he pulled out his wallet and sorted through it until he found his military I.D. card. He laid the card down in front of the girl. "Look at it. It's got my picture on it, see? Okay. Now, that's Harry," he pointed to the picture, "and *I'm* Harry. Now do you get it?"

Her face lit up. "Haa-lee," she said, and pointed first to the card and then to him. "Haa-lee!"

"Yeah! Yeah, now you got it! Harry. My name is Harry."

She turned to the others and said something, fast and sing-song, in Vietnamese. What a crazy mixed-up language! It wasn't any wonder that he couldn't speak it, with all that singing up and down every time you tried to say something.

"Mi," the girl said, and tapped her own chest.

"Huh?"

"Mi." She smiled at him. "Mi."

"Mi," repeated Harry, trying to say it the same way she did. "Your name is Mi. Beautiful. How about the rest of them? The little girl," and he pointed at her. "What's her name?"

"Bong," said Mi.

"Bong, huh? How about that. *Chao ong,* Bong."

Bong giggled and sucked on her fingers.

"Ton," said Mi, and gestured toward the boy. "Ton."

"*Chao ong,* Ton."

Ton just sat there, not smiling, not saying anything, not even moving. What the hell was the matter with the kid? You'd think he'd loosen up a little bit.

"How about the baby?" Harry asked Mi. "What's the baby's name?"

Mi looked at him, not understanding.

"The baby," repeated Harry, pointing. "Doesn't the baby have a name?"

Mi smiled and shook her head, telling him that she didn't understand what he was saying. Not that it made any difference, Harry thought. He didn't guess he'd be having too many conversations with the baby.

The rain stopped as suddenly as it had begun. And Harry's head was starting to ache—not bad, but enough to bug him. It was a sort of fuzzy feeling, really, like the time he'd spent three nights straight cramming for an algebra final and ended up straining his eyes so bad that he had to wear dark glasses for a week. Yeah, like that. Maybe he was coming down with something, like malaria. A lot of the guys ended up with malaria, and once you got it, you had it for the rest of your life, that's what the medics said; They handed out anti-malaria pills in the mess halls, but they were bummers; once you took the pills, you couldn't have a beer without getting sick, and so most of the guys let the pills alone and took their chances with the malaria.

Malaria, Harry thought. That's all I need.

He peered out of the shelter, trying to see where the sun was so that he could tell the time. Dusk. The sky was red and smoky-looking and the sun was out of sight below the trees. It would be dark soon.

It occurred to him that he hadn't eaten since before they'd started the patrol. Maybe *that* was why his head ached, maybe he was just hungry. Now that he thought about it, he realized that he was hungry, real hungry.

"How about some chow?" he asked Mi.

She gave him that questioning, I-don't-understand smile of hers. She was really kind of pretty, especially when she smiled.

He dug into his pack and pulled out all the C-rations he had, lining the little tin cans up on the ground between them. There was enough for a couple of days— tuna and noodles, corned beef, spaghetti, beans, peaches, hot dogs. "Whatever you want," Harry told Mi.

Mi just sat there, looking at the tins as if she didn't know what they were. She'd probably never seen food in tin cans before, living way out here in the middle of nowhere. He'd have to show her. Harry opened one of the tins—the tuna and noodles, these people were always eating noodles and he figured she'd like it—and held it out to Mi.

"It's food. Dinner. Go ahead, taste it."

She didn't move.

Harry reached for the booklet full of Useful Phrases, but by now it was too dark to read anything. "Listen to me. This is food. Good, healthy food. It's tuna and noodles, see? You've seen noodles before, haven't you? Well, these noodles are just like Vietnamese noodles, except that they've got tuna with them. Tuna is a fish. You know what a fish is, don't you? Look, watch me." Harry pantomimed eating, licking his lips and rubbing his stomach, and Bong laughed merrily.

"You get it? Okay," Harry said, and he pushed the open tin toward Mi. "Now you do it. Taste it. It won't hurt you."

Mi reached out, but then Ton said something, quick and sharp, and Mi jerked her hand back away from the tin as if it was full of rattlesnakes.

"What'd you have to go and do that for?" Harry asked Ton. "What's the matter with you, anyway? What'd you tell her? Did you tell her it was poisoned or something?"

Ton squatted there, glaring at Harry as if he'd like to stick a knife into his belly. Harry'd seen a line of prisoners once, on the way to interrogation, and that's how they'd been looking at the GI's who were guarding them. But Ton was just a kid.

"Okay. You think I'm trying to poison you, huh? Is that what you think? Then watch me." Dipping his fingers into the tin, Harry put a handful of the stuff into his mouth, chewed it and swallowed it. "There. See? I wouldn't be eating it if it was poisoned, would I?"

Ton said something, but this time Mi answered him back, her own voice as sharp as his. Then she took some of the food, just a little bit, and put it in her mouth as daintily as if it was a cream puff.

"It's good, isn't it? See? I told you it was all right. I'm just trying to be your friend, don't you understand that?"

Mi smiled.

Harry opened three more of the cans, and passed them around. Ton turned his back on them and wouldn't even answer Mi when she tried to talk to him, but Mi and Bong ate hungrily, as if they hadn't had anything to eat for a long time. Harry ate too, but it was strange; now that he had the food in his mouth, he wasn't nearly as hungry as he'd thought he was.

He was a little worried about the baby. It was still sleeping, but it would have to wake up sometime . . . and when it woke up, it was going to be hungry. Maybe it was Mi's baby, and she'd breast-feed it. She didn't look old enough to have a baby, but you could never tell. There was a twelve-year-old girl back home who'd had a baby; they'd put it up for adoption, of course, and sent the girl to reform school, but it was *possible,* that was the point.

Bong had eaten most of the peaches, and now she picked up the nearly-empty tin to drink the syrup. Mi said something gently, and took the tin away from the crestfallen little girl.

"Go ahead and let her have it," Harry told Mi. "It's sweet, and kids like sweet things. Go ahead. I don't want any more, honest."

Mi shook her head and put the tin down beside her leg, as if she planned to save it.

"It won't keep. The ants'll get at it or something. Let Bong have it."

Mi started to say something, then laughed and shook her head. Harry laughed too. They were all getting along pretty well, he thought, considering that they couldn't speak any English and he couldn't speak any Vietnamese.

His head was still bothering him. The food hadn't helped much, after all. Maybe he had a concussion. He'd heard stories about guys who got hit on the head and knocked out just the same as he had. They'd come to, those guys, and they'd be okay for a while, and then all of a sudden they'd drop dead.

Yeah, maybe. But it didn't help to think about it.

Bong yawned, and nestled close to Mi. What was he going to do with these kids? They must live around here. Didn't they have anywhere to go? Where had they slept *last* night, for Pete's sake?

He couldn't just throw them out, not after he'd fed them. It was dark now, and they were just kids. He couldn't let them go wandering around in the dark, it wouldn't be right.

The baby woke up and started to cry.

Mi cradled it on her lap, crooning to it. Then she dipped her fingers into the peach syrup that she'd saved, and let the baby suck the sweet, sugary stuff from her fingertips.

"Look at him go. He likes it," Harry said.

Mi smiled.

The baby finished the syrup, burped, and went back to sleep. Bong was asleep too, her head resting on Mi's leg. Ton squatted in his corner, motionless, his eyes like little bits of coal-fire in the darkness.

"He makes me nervous," Harry said to Mi.

Mi said nothing; he kept forgetting she couldn't understand him.

The first thing they taught you in survival school was this: Never take prisoners. They drummed it into you, again and again: Never take prisoners. The only good Vietnamese is a dead one.

So what am I supposed to do? Harry asked himself wearily. Shoot them? Shoot a girl and two kids and a baby?

He couldn't do it. He couldn't shoot kids. Even if he knew for a fact that they were working for Charlie . . . hell, it would be like committing murder.

You learned a lot of things in survival school, but none of them seemed to fit what was happening here and now. A guy had to make his own decisions. And Harry had decided. He couldn't shoot kids.

He could wake them up and tell them to leave, though. Yeah, he could do that. He could just tell them to get out of here, to go home. If they had a home.

Harry sighed. He could just imagine what the guys in his outfit would say if they could see him now. They'd say he was crazy. They'd say he was soft. Okay. Maybe he *was* soft. There were worse things than being soft.

He'd have to sit up all night, that was all there was to it. So long as he stayed awake, everything would be okay. Quietly, Harry shifted his pack around so that he was leaning against it, and then he reached out and drew the M-16 close to him, where he could keep his hands on it.

Tomorrow, when it was light, he'd figure out what to do about the kids.

It wouldn't be the first time he'd stayed up all night.

They were already asleep, all four of them, breathing slowly and evenly in the darkness. Poor kids . . . it must be rough to grow up in a country that's been at war for twenty years.

Sitting there, he figured that he'd done the right thing. They were just kids. The worst they could do was to steal his gear, and they couldn't even do that, just as long as he stayed awake . . .

# FOUR

"Now's the time to do it," said Ton. "While he's asleep."

"To do what?"

"To kill him. What else?"

"Oh, Ton!" As weary and as confused as she was, Ton's dramatics irritated her. Why couldn't he understand that this wasn't a game? "If you'd just keep quiet and let me think for a minute . . ."

"What's there to think about? If we don't kill him, he'll kill us."

"If he was going to kill us, he could have done it before now."

"Maybe he wants to take us back to his base and torture us. That's what they do. They tie you up, and then they attach electric wires to . . ."

"Ton, keep quiet!"

Mi's eyes burned with unshed tears and weariness. She could never remember having been as tired as she was now. Never. Her hands trembled and her body ached and there was a strange, stale taste in her mouth.

For a while, she'd thought that the American soldier would *never* go to sleep. Feigning sleep themselves, she and Ton had struggled to stay awake. They had not dared to move or to whisper to one another until the American had begun to snore, and even then it had seemed to take forever for them to edge their way past Bong and Little Brother and the sprawled-out American soldier who called himself Haa-lee, to creep across the grass to this place several hundred meters away from the shelter.

"It will be quick, like this!" Ton said, snapping his fingers.

"And suppose he wakes up? What then?"

"He won't wake up. I'll hit him with a rock, and then I'll take his gun away from him and shoot him with it."

"You will not."

"He killed Mama," Ton said, in a strange, choking voice. "If Papa was here . . ."

"Well, Papa's not here." Mi hesitated. "*He* didn't kill Mama. He's just a soldier, Ton. And I think he's lost."

"Lost? Why do you think that?"

"I don't know, I just do. And I'll tell you what else I think. I think he's just as scared of us as we are of him."

"*I'm* not scared of him."

"He's awfully young," mused Mi.

"How can you tell how old he is?"

"By looking at him."

"They all look the same to me," muttered Ton. "With their big noses and their round eyes. Like big, pale fish. Hung Ba used to call them foreign devils."

Mi closed her eyes. Hung Ba! If it hadn't been for

Hung Ba and his endless intrigues with the silent men who came and went by night, their village might have been spared and they might be sleeping in their own beds tonight. Hung Ba! And where had all of his fine ideas about politics and war and independence finally led him? To a horrible, ignominious death, a death that had gobbled up not only Hung Ba, but the entire village. Hung Ba indeed!

"Hung Ba was a fool."

"He wasn't! He *knew* this would happen, he said . . ."

"Of course he knew! It was his fault! If he hadn't meddled in things that were none of his business, the Americans might have left us alone!"

Oh! It would be so good to lie down, to sleep.

Far away, thunder rumbled . . . or perhaps it was bombs. Mi didn't know. I must decide, she thought. I must decide what we are going to do.

"I'd rather be dead than be a prisoner."

"We're not prisoners," replied Mi.

"We will be, if we don't kill him. They might even send us to Con Son."

"Con Son is for political prisoners. We're not political prisoners. Stop talking nonsense."

"It's not nonsense. Suppose the American said that we were political prisoners? Suppose he said that we were from the North? Look at what happened in Long Ton."

Mi didn't know anything about what had happened in Long Ton, and she said so.

"The American soldiers marched in, and there was nobody to stop them. First they burned down all the huts. Then they made everyone stand out in the road. There were only three men in the village, and two of them were so old that they couldn't even stand up without help. But that didn't make any difference to the Americans. They just went and shot them, like pigs. Right in front of everybody. And then they made all the rest of the people get into trucks, and they sealed up the trucks and they took them to the prison camps in Gia Long." Ton's voice shook with indignation. "They wouldn't give them food, or water, or medicine, or anything. And do you know why they did it? It was because they said that all of the people in Long Ton were communists, that's why."

One of Hung Ba's stories, thought Mi. Maybe it was true and maybe it wasn't. "Well, maybe they were communists," she said.

"A whole village full of communists? Who ever heard of such a thing?"

"I don't know. Neither do you. Ton, please let me think."

"There's nothing to think about. We've got to kill him." Ton was silent for a moment. "Women don't understand these things. Let me do it, Mi. You can close your eyes and put your fingers in your ears, if you want to."

"Close your own eyes!" snapped Mi angrily. "Put your own fingers in your own ears! And while you're at it, you might put a coconut in your mouth, too. Anything to stop your yap-yap-yapping! Kill, kill, kill—can't you think of anything else?"

Ton was silent, sulking. Mi didn't care.

But perhaps Ton was right. Who could tell what the American might do? They were unpredictable. It wasn't wise to trust them. If they killed the American—shot him while he slept—then certainly he wouldn't be able to harm them. They could take his gun and his food and his boots and trade them for food in the next village.

Mi turned toward the shelter, then hesitated. Ton's eyes watched her. "What are we going to do then?"

"I don't know," said Mi.

"It'll be light soon."

"Yes."

But the American had told them to come in out of the rain. He had tried to talk to them in their own language. He had shared his food with them. If he'd wanted to kill them, surely he'd have done it before now . . .

"We could sell his gun," Ton said. "And his boots, too. The people would say we were heroes."

"It doesn't take courage to kill a sleeping man. A fine pair of heroes we'd be!"

Mi had never heard of an American speaking Vietnamese. Of course he hadn't really been speaking, he'd been reading words from a book. But he was trying to talk to us, Mi thought. He was trying to speak our language.

Mi closed her eyes, and rubbed at them with her fingertips.

*If she killed the American while he slept, she would be no different than the men who destroyed their village.*

The thought came unbidden and unwanted, like a cry or an evil omen. Mi shivered in the chill of dawn. Right. Wrong. There was no answer, and it grew lighter by the moment. She felt . . . she didn't know what she felt, that was the trouble. She did not know.

A bird sang out, just once, and was silent.

"No," said Mi. "We can't kill him."

"But why not?"

"Because it would be murder. And we are not murderers, you and I."

"War is murder."

"Perhaps. But we are not soldiers, either."

4 3

"You're afraid," accused Ton.

Yes, she was afraid. But not of the American, thought Mi. I am afraid of myself, of the person I must become if I am to kill . . .

It was not something that was easily explained to an excited nine-year-old boy.

"No, we won't kill him. We don't have to kill him. We were going to go to Saigon, remember? We were going to find Papa. It was *your* idea," Mi added.

She couldn't remember whose idea it had been, but she hoped to take Ton's thoughts away from the American soldier; perhaps it *had* been Ton's idea . . . it didn't matter.

"But what about the American?"

Mi shrugged. "What about him? We'll leave right now, while he's still asleep."

"And when he wakes up, he'll go running back to his army and tell them all about us."

"What if he does? We'll be miles away by that time. Besides, what could he tell them? That he'd seen a girl and some children? That he gave us some food? It doesn't make a very exciting story, does it?"

Ton was silent, eyes cast down. Mi watched him, but held her tongue. She would let him think it through, she would let him persuade himself that her plan was better than his. It was best not to bully Ton.

"I'd rather kill him. I'm not afraid."

"Of course you're not afraid! Don't you think I know that? It isn't a question of being afraid, though. We can't just think of ourselves, we have to think of Bong and Little Brother. Suppose we kill him. What do you think would happen to us?

"I'll tell you what would happen," Mi went on, not giving Ton a chance to interrupt. "Because I've thought about it, even if you haven't. Certainly this American soldier's comrades are searching for him. Sooner or later, they would find him—murdered. And then they would come looking for us, and when they found us . . ."

"I didn't think of that."

"Well think of it now!"

"Perhaps they're already looking for him," Ton said uneasily.

"Perhaps. And if they are, the sound of a gun being fired would bring them right here, right to this spot! You say that you're not afraid to die, but what about Bong? What about Little Brother? What do you suppose the Americans would do to them?"

Ton stood before her, chastened and frightened, and Mi felt guilty and wondered if perhaps she'd gone too far.

No, she decided. Hung Ba's recklessness had set a poor example. Now, Ton must learn that courage disciplined itself with reason.

"But what about his gun? Can't we take it away from him? At least then we'd be able to defend ourselves."

Mi hesitated. The gun would be useful. Not only might it serve as a weapon, but when they reached Quan Long they could surely sell it for enough *piasters* to buy their way to Saigon.

"It's just lying there on his lap," said Ton eagerly. "All I have to do is reach down—like this—and take it. The Americans have lots of guns . . ."

"What if he wakes up?"

"He won't wake up."

Before she could protest or even think it through properly, Ton was gone, moving swiftly across the tall, dew-dampened grasses and then vanishing in the shadowy bamboo thickets that surrounded the clearing.

"Ton . . ."

But he did not hear, or else he did not choose to hear.

Sighing, Mi settled back to wait for Ton. It was so dark and so still. It could not be many minutes before sunrise, and yet the night was as black as if it would last forever. She shivered, and crossed her arms for warmth.

She ought to have stopped Ton. It was foolishness to risk death for a gun that was only worth a handful of *piasters!* She'd have called him back if she'd dared to, but to call out now would surely awaken the American.

The utter silence pressed upon her ears and made her feel dizzy. The whole world seemed to be holding its breath, waiting . . . waiting.

It was *too* quiet. Sudden apprehension sent waves of nausea through her body. It was too quiet. In a moment, something would happen. American soldiers, hundreds of them, moving through the jungle and along the river banks, coming closer and closer, surrounding them with guns and bayonets and gigantic clattering machines that spat fire and death . . .

Her heart seemed to rise into her throat, and she could scarcely breathe.

A slow, suffocating minute passed. Nothing happened. The silence seemed to invade Mi's body, filling her ears and eyes and lungs, mingling with her blood so that it was as if she were actually breathing it . . . and nothing happened.

The wild terror that she felt ebbed slowly away. It was always quiet just before dawn. For now, at least, there was nothing to fear.

How long had Ton been gone? A minute? Five minutes? Mi peered into the darkness, but she could see nothing save the shadowy clumps of bamboo, black tracings upon the gray sky. It was getting lighter. A few minutes ago, she hadn't been able to see the bamboo.

Bong and the baby. Sleeping. Suppose they woke up? Should she go and get them? The baby would be hungry by now, hungry and wet and angry at the whole world for neglecting him . . . suppose the baby began to cry?

To her left, the bushes rustled just a little bit. An animal, perhaps. Mi caught her breath and waited. Silence. No human being could be so still; it must have been an animal, some small, nocturnal creature that sought shelter from the coming heat and light of day.

And then a twig snapped, sharp as a pistol-shot in the stillness. Mi gasped.

"It's just me. Did I scare you?"

"Ton!" Angry at his game-playing, Mi took a step toward him. She made her voice stern. "Why did you sneak up on me like that?"

"I'd make a pretty good guerrilla fighter, wouldn't I? Do you want to know something? I was watching you for a whole minute and you didn't even know I was there! If you'd been an American soldier, I'd have killed you before you even knew it!" Ton was wearing the machine-gun just as Haa-lee had worn it, slung over his shoulder. "How do I look? Do I look like an American?"

"You look like a small boy carrying a large gun," snapped Mi, still angry with him. "You'd have done better to get some food, as long as you were out stealing."

"But I did! I got lots of things, that's what took so long. He was sleeping on top of his knapsack, but I got my hand in under the flap and pulled out as much as I could. I got a flashlight, and matches, and little cans of food and medicines in a white tin box, and chocolate and . . ."

"But where is it?"

"I took it all down to the river."

Mi almost wept with exasperation. "Why did you take it down to the river? Why didn't you bring it back here? You knew I was waiting for you and worrying about you!"

"I didn't mean for you to be worried, Mi. But I thought that as long as we were going to cross the river, I might as well take everything down there so it would be waiting for us when we got there. You'll be carrying Little Brother, and I'll be carrying the gun—it's awfully heavy, much heavier than it looks—and I just thought . . ."

"All right, all right." He looked so crestfallen, standing there with a gun that was almost as big as he was, that Mi's heart went out to him. "You did the right thing. You did a good job."

Ton beamed at her.

"Are the children still asleep?"

Ton nodded.

"And the American?"

"He's sleeping too. He makes noises when he sleeps, like an old man." Ton shut his mouth and filled his cheeks with air, breathing noisily through his nose. "Like that."

Mi giggled.

"Do you think they *all* sleep like that?"

"I don't know," said Mi. "Maybe. Some of their customs are very strange—at least that's what Papa says."

"I'll be glad when we find Papa."

"So will I."

Already the sky was gray. They would have to hurry.

"We'll have to go back and get Bong and the baby," Mi said. "But what will we do with your gun?"

"I'll go. You'd make too much noise."

Mi started to protest, but nodded instead. Ton had proved that he could move through the swamp as quietly as a puff of wind; it would be safer for all of them if he went alone.

"Give me the gun, then."

Ton handed it across to her, and she staggered beneath its weight. "It must weigh ten kilos! How did you manage to carry it?"

"I can carry lots more than that," boasted Ton. "I can carry twenty kilos on my back all day, and never get tired. Once, I carried twenty-five kilos for three hours, without resting. And one time . . ."

"When was this?" Mi asked curiously.

Ton gave her a strange, sheepish look.

"Hung Ba?" guessed Mi.

Ton nodded. "He was training us. He'd fill an empty sack with rocks, and then he'd tie it to our shoulders, like a pack. We'd have contests, to see who could carry the most weight, and who could go the longest time without resting."

Mi stared. "You and who else?"

"All of the boys. And some of the girls, too. The ones we could trust."

"But . . . *why?*"

"Hung Ba said that someday we'd have to fight the Americans. He wanted us to be ready."

Mi simply looked at him, too astounded to say anything further.

"I'll go and get the baby," said Ton.

He set out across the clearing, and this time, Mi could follow his progress all the way to the bamboo. It was truly something to see, the way he moved across the grass without making a sound, quietly as a shadow. He might have been a ghost or a man-shaped mist, instead of a boy. Had

Hung Ba taught him this, too?

Ton returned within minutes, carrying the sleeping baby.

"Good!" Mi lay the machine-gun down in the grass and took the child into her arms. "He didn't wake up . . . and look how wet he is! Poor little fellow!"

"He felt hot."

"That's nothing. Babies always feel hot."

"Are you sure?" asked Ton.

"Of course I'm sure."

"I thought maybe he might be sick."

"Why should he be sick?" Mi asked impatiently. "He was all right last night. He's just sleepy, aren't you?" she asked the baby, who stirred and gurgled in her arms.

"Now I'll go back and get Bong."

"Well, be careful. Don't frighten her."

Ton eyed the gun. "You shouldn't just leave it lying there on the ground," he said reproachfully. "It'll get rusty."

"It doesn't matter. We'll sell it when we get to Quan Long."

"But I wanted to keep it," protested Ton.

"What for?"

"Well . . . because I captured it."

Games again! thought Mi angrily. "You didn't capture it. You stole it from a sleeping man."

Ton gave the gun a lingering, wistful look.

"Go and get Bong," said Mi.

Wordlessly, Ton went.

While he was gone, Mi changed the baby, hiding his wet clothes in the reeds and tearing a piece of cloth from her own sleeve so that she could make him a new garment. It was strange that he slept so soundly. He ought to be very hungry by now. Perhaps he *was* sick.

Touching the baby's forehead with her fingertips, Mi frowned.

Ton returned then, carrying Bong, who was rubbing her eyes sleepily and getting ready to ask questions.

"Hush!" whispered Mi, putting her forefinger on Bong's lips. She turned to Ton. "Is the American still sleeping?"

Ton nodded.

"Then let's go. It'll be light soon, and he certainly won't sleep much past sunrise!"

Throughout most of the year, the river was as wide and as shallow as any paddy, a slow-moving, sluggish ribbon of muddy water in which the women washed clothes and occasionally bathed. It wasn't a very good river for fishing; the children who splashed in the shallows had long since scared away all but the tiniest fish.

Now, however, the usually placid currents were swollen and angry, and the gray waters seethed and hissed as if some evil spirit had built a fire beneath them. The monsoon had come early this year.

Mi had forgotten about the monsoon.

She stood there on the muddy river bank, holding the baby on her shoulder, wanting to cry. Ton looked up at her expectantly. She was the eldest. She must decide what they would do next.

"We can't cross here. It's too deep, and the currents are dangerous."

"But we *have* to cross here," replied Ton.

There was fear in his voice. Mi smiled, to reassure him.

"No we don't. We'll go downstream. There's a foot-bridge in Vinh Luc."

"The Americans bombed Vinh Luc two weeks ago."

"But the bridge is outside of town. And it's only a footbridge, just a few pieces of bamboo. Perhaps they left it alone."

"It's twenty kilometers to Vinh Luc," said Ton, "and the American soldier will come after us as soon as he wakes up and sees that we took his gun."

Mi was close to tears. "But look at the river! We'd never be able to get across—it's too deep!"

"Maybe it's not as deep as it looks." Before Mi could stop him, Ton had waded into the river. Dodging the sticks and bits of debris that were being carried downstream, he managed to make his way halfway across. "See? It's not even up to my shoulders!"

Mi motioned him back.

The eastern sky was pink and gold and amber, and Mi knew that the sun would rise above the shimmering horizon at any moment. All over the swamp, birds were singing. Even now, the American named Haa-lee might be stirring, waking up, realizing that they'd stolen his gun and his supplies . . .

The supplies. She gazed at them—a bulky, unwieldy bundle lashed together with vines, lying in the mud at her feet. Ton would have to carry them.

"Will we try it?" asked Ton.

It would never occur to the American that they'd crossed here. He would not try to follow them, because he would not know where they had gone. They would be safe on the other side of the river.

Ton picked up the bundled provisions, and slung them over his shoulder.

"Wait," said Mi. "I'll go first."

Holding the baby high against her body, Mi knelt down and told Bong to climb up on her shoulders, just as if they were going to have a game of boy-and-bullock.

Bong laughed at the thought of games before breakfast, and did as she was told. So far, so good.

"Put your arms around my neck," said Mi. "Not so tight—you're choking me. There, like that. Now hold on. We don't want you to fall into the river, do we?"

"I'm hungry," said Bong. "I want some rice. And some yellow fruit, like we had last night."

"Later. After we cross the river."

The first rays of morning sunshine were filtering through the thick foliage of bamboo and areca palm. Even now, they might be too late. Suppose Haa-lee were to come running along the river bank, shouting at them to come back?

Getting a good grip on the baby, Mi steadied herself and waded slowly into the swift, muddy water.

# FIVE

He didn't know what it was that had awakened him, but he was on his feet in an instant, staring around the empty shelter and knowing that he'd been tricked.

Lousy, stinking little brats!

They were gone all right. And it looked as if they'd taken everything they could carry with them, the ungrateful, thieving, slant-eyed gooks. Breathing hard, and so mad that he hardly knew what he was doing, Harry smashed into the support-pole of the shelter with his fist, bringing it down in a heap of torn and tangled vines.

It was his own fault, his own stupid fault. Those guys at survival school knew what they were talking about. Never give a gook an even break. Good old soft-hearted

Harry . . . *soft-headed,* that's what he was. Yeah. Well, next time he'd know better.

Kneeling down, Harry pawed through the wreckage of the shelter, looking to see if they'd left anything behind. The M-16 was gone, along with his extra clips of ammunition. They'd got the grenades, too. Sneaky little bastards, he should have shot them while he still had the chance.

Harry shook his head, disgusted with himself. The funny part of it was, he'd liked them. He'd really liked them. He'd wanted to help them, too. And this was the thanks he got for being decent.

At least they hadn't got his knapsack. Feeling a little better, Harry undid the flaps and opened it, groped inside and then flung it down on the ground. He didn't know how they'd done it, but just about everything was gone. First Aid kit, C-rations, flares, matches, salt tablets, water purifiers, the works. They'd done a nice thorough job, he had to hand it to them.

He suddenly wondered why they hadn't shot him, while they were at it. It would have been a damn sight safer. They probably hadn't been able to figure out how to work the M-16. Stupid, thieving gooks.

How long had he been asleep? A couple of minutes? An hour? All night?

They must have been planning it right from the beginning. Yeah. That's what they'd been jabbering about, knowing damn well that he couldn't speak Vietnamese and couldn't understand what they were saying. That girl, looking at him with those big, innocent eyes and all the while figuring out how she was going to rob him . . . it was sickening, that's what it was.

She'd have a great future on Tu Do Street, Harry

thought contemptuously. He could just see her, sitting in one of those little bars, swinging her legs and drinking her Saigon Tea and bilking some poor GI out of three months' pay. Yeah, she'd do just fine.

He stood up. He wanted a cigarette; he took the pack out of his shirt pocket, then reconsidered. He still had half a dozen matches in his belt pouch, but it might be a good idea to hang onto them. Drawing his arm back, he threw the cigarettes as far as he could into the silent jungle.

Far away, he heard a rooster crow. A *rooster,* Harry thought. Way out here in the middle of nowhere—a rooster! Must be a village or something. No, there weren't supposed to be any villages. Not out here. All of this country belonged to Charlie.

The sun was up over the treetops now, and it was getting hot. Well, what now? There wasn't much point in trying to track them down. No telling how much head start they'd had. Probably they'd taken off as soon as he'd closed his eyes. Yeah. But if he ever got his hands on them . . .

Then he heard it, and stood very still, listening. Voices.

Harry held his breath. But now, the jungle was oddly quiet. He waited. He was *sure* that he'd heard something. A slow minute passed. Harry shrugged. He must have been hearing things, he decided.

No use standing around here. Slowly, Harry moved through the grass, heading east. He was unarmed, except for a pocketknife, and those kids had probably already told Charlie where he was. Well, he was ready for anything—a trick, an ambush, anything. They might take him, but they wouldn't take him without a fight.

He was already sweating. Too bad about those salt

tablets. And water—what was he going to do for drinking water? Not to mention food. It was a mess, all right. A lousy, stinking mess.

A wall of high-growing, vine-laced bushes that were tall enough to be trees blocked his way. Miserable, lousy jungle. Harry started to work his way around the thicket, then changed his mind and lowered his head, as if he was back in high school making a tackle, and smashed his way through the woven-together leaves and vines, making one hell of a racket and not caring.

Okay, Charlie. Now you know where I am. So what are you going to do about it? he asked silently. What are you going to do about it?

A few steps farther, the ground sloped muddily down to the edge of a river. Even from here, Harry could see that the current was fast and tricky, breaking up into little whirlpools and eddies and carrying big branches downstream as easily as if they'd been made of paper. They wouldn't have been able to get across, Harry figured, not with all that gear. There wasn't any bridge in sight. Wherever they were, they were still on this side of the river.

Looking down at the rushing, tumbling gray waters, Harry remembered that it was almost time for the monsoon to start. Yeah, that's why the river was running so high and so fast—monsoon. In a couple of weeks, this whole area would be under water. Not that it made any difference to the local people; they actually looked forward to the floods. They built their houses on stilts so that they could raise up the floors, and then the whole family just sat around and waited for the water to go down.

Man, it was hard to believe that people could live in the twentieth century and still be as backward and ignorant as the average Vietnamese peasant, with his bullock and his wooden plow. They were still in the Dark Ages, except for a few of the educated ones who lived in the cities.

Those kids! They'd probably known about the river all along! Maybe they'd decided to follow it to a town or something. But which way would they have gone? Not upstream; the bank dwindled out to nothing and the water was already high enough to be drowning some of the bamboo along the river bank. It was a cinch they hadn't gone upstream.

Harry turned and looked down the river. About twenty-five yards from where he stood, the river dog-legged around an outcropping stand of banana trees. There was no telling what lay beyond the bend. It might be a town, it might be a bridge, it might be anything.

Still, it was worth a try. And the river bank, even though it was muddy, was easier going than the jungle.

Slowly, Harry made his way toward the banana trees. The mud was soft and kind of slimy and it smelled bad, like rotten fish or moldy old clothes in the bottom of a closet. It made a lot more sense, Harry found, to simply walk in the river itself.

He splashed along, trying not to make too much noise. What a country! Between the mud and the stink and the mosquitoes and the leeches . . . what a crazy place to fight a war!

He was just a couple of steps from the banana trees when he heard it, a girl yelling something in Vietnamese, yelling it over and over again. It was her all right.

Excited now, Harry waded straight out toward the

sharpest point of the outcrop, figuring it to be the short-
est distance between where he was and where the girl
was. The water wasn't as deep as he'd thought it would
be—just a little past his waist—but the river bottom was
rocky and full of sinkholes, and the current was strong
enough to throw him off balance if he wasn't careful.

He came abreast of the banana trees and then he saw
her, right there in the middle of the river and nearly up
to her neck in water. So they'd tried to cross the river
after all, the stupid little gooks! The girl was holding
the baby up as high as she could, and swaying back and
forth. Harry figured that she must have blundered into
a sinkhole. Bong was riding on her shoulders, clinging
to her neck like a scared monkey.

"Thought you'd get away with it, huh?"

Mi tried to turn her head far enough to see him, but
she couldn't. Harry waded toward her, grinning.

"What did you do with my gear?" he asked.

He was close enough to touch her now; close enough
to see the drops of water and perspiration on her forehead, even close enough to see her eyelashes and the
round, black pupils of her eyes. She looked scared. Well,
she *ought* to be scared.

"All right, give me the baby."

She hesitated.

"Come on, come on. Give me the baby. I'm not going
to hurt it."

She stared at him for what seemed like a long time,
and then she let him take the baby away from her.

He hoisted the baby to his shoulder. It hardly weighed
anything at all, and it didn't make a sound. Maybe it
was sick. Maybe it was starving to death . . .

"Come on. You can't cross the river here, you dumb

gook. If you try it, you'll drown. So be a nice girl, and show me where you put my gear."

She started to say something, but he cut her short.

"Never mind. You just come with me and show me where you hid my gear."

Turning his back on her, he splashed his way back to shore. She ought to be able to make it on her own, he figured, now that her hands were free. But where was the other one, the boy?

He put the baby down on a clump of grass, clumsily. Babies made him nervous.

Harry turned back to the river and scowled. Mi was still standing in the middle of the river, right there where he'd left her. What was the matter with her anyway?

"Come on back here! The baby's hungry!"

She gave him a sort of frantic look, but she didn't move. Quicksand? Maybe he ought to go in after her. But that would mean leaving the baby all by itself. "What's the matter? Are you stuck?"

From atop Mi's shoulders, Bong raised her arm and pointed downstream.

All that was visible of Ton was his head and his two arms. He had almost made it to the far side of the river, but now he was up to his neck in water and holding the M-16 as high as he could above his head.

Harry grinned. Served him right, the little smart-fart. Maybe this would teach him not to go around stealing guns from American GIs.

Ton twisted around, and Harry saw that the water was up over his mouth, splashing into his face.

He could swim for it, if he'd just let go of the gun.

But Ton was obviously not going to let go of the gun. The kid's got guts, Harry thought.

Plunging back into the river, Harry let the current carry him downstream until he was almost on top of Ton.

"Okay, kid. The party's over. Give me the gun."

But to Harry's surprise, Ton clung to the weapon as if it was a life line. You wouldn't think such a skinny little kid would have so much strength in his hands.

"Come on, kid. What are you going to do with an M-16? You don't even know how to make it work. Come on, let go of it—I said, *let go!*"

Harry yanked and fell backwards, but he got the gun away from Ton. Man! That was one stubborn kid! If he'd just been a couple of inches taller, he might have gotten away with it, M-16 and all.

Ton was treading water now, treading water and glaring up at Harry like an animal that knows it's trapped and expects to be killed.

"Can you swim?"

Ton lifted his head clear of the water, and spat.

Shifting the M-16 to his left hand, Harry hauled off and let the little brat have it, hard, right in the chops. Ton toppled and went under.

Mi screamed.

Later, Harry figured that it must have been just at that moment that Bong fell into the river. He'd waited to make sure that Ton was okay—he didn't want to kill the kid, just teach him some manners—and then when he'd turned around to tell Mi that her brother was okay and to shut up the yelling, he'd realized that Bong was . . . well, gone. Like she'd disappeared into thin air.

And that was what Mi was screaming about.

Harry just stood there, up to his waist in water, staring at Mi's shoulders as if he could somehow bring Bong back just by looking at the place where she'd been.

He couldn't move. He couldn't think. It was almost like being paralyzed. And then whatever it was snapped, and without even thinking about it, he tossed the M-16 away and dove.

He couldn't see a thing. He groped along the stony river bottom, stretching his arms out as far as he could to either side, figuring that Bong would be pushed downstream by the current and hoping that he could grab her as she came past him. It wasn't any good. Lungs bursting, he came up for air.

Way over to his right, Bong's head suddenly bobbed above water. He saw her open her mouth, trying to get a breath of air, and then she went under again and Harry went after her.

This time, he stayed under until he thought he'd pass out, and then at the last minute he touched something that might have been Bong's leg and grabbed hold of it and dragged it up with him. He had her! He got her up into his arms. She was unconscious, a limp little bundle of skin and bones and wet rags. Her head was bleeding.

Mi was struggling toward him.

"Never mind! We've got to get her to shore!"

He headed back toward where he'd left the baby, and this time, Mi followed him.

Gently, he laid Bong down on the spongy ground. She wasn't breathing. Mi knelt beside Bong, her eyes as big as saucers, and scared.

"I think her leg's broken, but that doesn't matter. We've got to get the water out of her lungs, we've got to get her breathing. You understand?"

Being as gentle as he could, Harry flipped Bong face down over his knee, so that her head was lower than her feet. The last time he'd done anything like this was in Boy Scouts . . . he hoped he was doing it right. There wouldn't be time for a second chance. He patted Bong's back a couple of times, not too hard, and a little bit of water trickled out of her mouth.

"You always got to get the water out of the lungs first. Otherwise, you drown 'em."

He was talking out loud, as much for his own sake as for Mi's.

"That ought to do it. Now I'll try to make her start breathing. Artificial respiration, understand?"

Working quickly, he laid Bong down on her back and pushed her chin up, tilting her head as far back as he could. She was as slender and fragile as a little bird. Bending over her, he breathed into her nose and mouth, trying to pace himself to his natural breathing.

Again and again. It wasn't any good. She wasn't breathing. She was too little, she was too young, she'd been under water too long. It wasn't any good.

Keep it up for as long as two hours. That's what Mr. O'Hara had told them, Harry remembered. Mr. O'Hara was the scoutmaster. Don't give up. You have a human life in your hands, you have a responsibility. Don't give up.

Mi was crying now, softly. It was as if someone was crying far, far away.

Don't give up. Inhale. Wait. Exhale. Inhale again.

Mi had stopped crying and there was silence, complete silence in which the rushing sound of the river and even the rhythmic sound of his own breathing seemed impossibly loud.

Bong hadn't moved.

The muscles in his calves and shoulders and back began to ache. Relax. He couldn't relax. Relax, or you'll cramp up. Take it easy. Inhale. Exhale. You've got all the time in the world. Don't give up.

Bong coughed, struggled for breath, coughed again. "She's breathing! Do you see that? She's breathing!" Bong opened her eyes, and Mi started to cry again.

"She'll be okay now."

Harry sat back on his haunches, grinning. He'd really thought the kid was a goner, over the hill . . .

Someone behind him, sneaking up on him. He could feel danger even when his back was turned, even when he was thinking about Bong being alive instead of dead . . . he could *feel* it, like a coldness in the pit of his stomach or a bad memory. They taught you how to smell danger and death in survival school; they taught you with live ammunition and with beatings and with hunger and with misery, they taught you so you'd never forget.

Okay then. If that was how it had to be, he was ready.

He leaped back and away, just managing to dodge the rock that was coming down on the back of his head. It glanced off his shoulder, not hard enough to break any bones but hard enough to hurt like the blazes. Only it didn't hurt until later.

"You little . . .!"

Not hearing, not caring, not seeing anything except that once again he'd failed to kill the American soldier, Ton leaped for his throat. Like a cat, Harry thought. Like a biting, yowling cat.

So easily it was almost a joke, Harry grabbed him and held both of his wrists in one hand. Ton kicked out and tried to bite, but he was a light-weight. Hell, it was like fighting with a kindergartener.

"Come on, kid. Settle down."

Ton struggled. Mi said something pleadingly.

"What am I supposed to do with him?" Harry asked her, more exasperated than angry. "If I let him go, he's just going to turn around and heave another rock at me as soon as my back's turned. So what do I have to do? Tie him up, maybe?"

Mi said something else, and Ton went suddenly as limp as a sack of potatoes. Bong lay quietly, watching them. Harry's shoulder started to hurt.

Mi was still talking to Ton, slow and easy, and Ton seemed to be listening. Harry wondered what she was saying. She was probably telling him about Bong, and about how Harry had saved her life.

What a mess. What a stinking mess! What now? Harry wondered morosely. A girl and three little kids—one of them with a busted leg and one of them ready to bash his brains in—and they were his responsibility. This was really one for the books—except nothing like this ever happened in the books.

"Haa-lee."

He looked at Mi. "Yeah?"

But that was the only English word she knew. Haa-lee. Harry. His name.

"You want me to let go of him? Is that what you want?"

Harry gazed down at Ton. What the hell, a half-pint like that wasn't going to do any damage.

"Okay, but just for you," said Harry, and he let go of Ton's wrists. Ton took a couple of steps backward, head down. Harry braced, but nothing happened.

"Mi, listen to me. I'm letting him get away with it this time but the next time he tries it, I'm going to kill him." Harry scowled, and drew his forefinger slowly and meaningfully across his throat. "You got that?"

She was staring at him, and her lower lip was trembling as if she was about to cry.

"Okay," said Harry. He didn't want her to cry. "Just

so we understand one another.''

Bong had begun to whimper very quietly.

That leg must be hurting her something fierce, Harry thought. Kneeling beside her, he ran his fingers lightly over the skin. Simple fracture. Lucky.

"I'm going to set Bong's leg," Harry said to Mi. "And it'll hurt. She'll cry. Maybe if we're lucky, she'll pass out. But it'll be a lot worse if I don't set it, do you understand? Do you *understand?*"

He groped on the ground, found a twig, broke it. He laid the broken stick on the ground, and then looked up to see if Mi was paying attention. She was. She was watching every move he made, intently. Trying to understand, thought Harry.

"Now, pay attention. This stick," and he pointed at the stick, "is broken the same way as Bong's leg is broken. Do you follow me?" He pointed at the stick, and then pointed at Bong's leg.

Mi frowned, then nodded.

Harry took the two pieces of the stick in his hands and straightened them.

Suddenly, Mi smiled. She gave Harry a solemn, searching look, and then took a resolute step backward, as if she'd made up her mind to trust him, to leave Bong in his hands.

He figured that she understood.

Crossing the clearing, Harry cut off a couple of lengths of bamboo and split them with his pocketknife. Mi had picked up the baby, and now she and Ton squatted side by side, watching everything he did. It was creepy, Harry thought, the way they just hunkered down and *stared* at a guy.

He laid the bamboo splints down alongside Bong, and

then hacked off several lengths of vine with which to bind the splints in place.

Bong lay perfectly still, but her eyes were open and scared.

Mi spoke then. Bong turned her head, and listened. She started to cry in earnest, but Mi just kept talking and in a few minutes, Bong was sniffing back the tears and even smiling a little bit.

Harry didn't know what was going on. Maybe Mi was telling Bong what was going to happen, that it was for her own good. He hoped so. But he didn't know.

Before he did anything, he took a good long look at the leg. At the most, it wouldn't take more than a minute to put the two bone ends together, and that would be the worst part. But sixty seconds of pain was a lot, Harry thought, especially for such a little kid.

Well, here goes.

As gently as he could, he took hold of Bong's leg and straightened it. He actually heard the bone go *click!* into place. Bong gave one sharp little cry, and then it was over. To his embarrassment, Harry's hands were shaking. He put them palms down on the soggy ground for a couple of seconds to steady them.

Ton and Mi hadn't moved.

Splinting the leg was a cinch. It was one of the things they'd learned to do in survival school, although Harry had known how to splint a leg since he was nine years old. It must have hurt some, but Bong never made a sound. Mild shock, maybe. He looped the vines around the bamboo and tied them. Bong didn't make a sound. But behind him, Harry heard Mi say something to Ton, softly.

He sat back and looked critically at his handiwork.

Not bad, he thought. Almost professional. He'd once thought that he wanted to be a doctor, but his family hadn't even been able to send him to college, much less medical school, and then Uncle Sam had come along and made the decision for him.

The baby began to whimper, and Mi shushed it.

Harry smiled at her. "Where'd you hide my gear?"

She gave him a blank, uncomprehending look.

"My gear, my food, the stuff that was in my pack. Come on, I know you took it. What did you do with it?"

Mi and Ton held a brief discussion. Lots of hand-waving and sing-songing, but nothing that made any sense to Harry. Then Mi handed the baby to Ton, stood up, and motioned Harry to follow her.

"Are you going to show me where you hid it? Is that the idea?"

Ton said something. Mi ignored him. She took a couple of steps, hesitated, looked at him. Harry didn't move.

"How do I know that this isn't another one of your little tricks?"

Of course he *didn't* know. That was the point. And you couldn't trust these people. Not even the kids. You couldn't trust them for a minute, no matter how nice and friendly they acted to your face, no matter what you did for them, no matter how nice you tried to treat them. You just couldn't trust them.

Mi was standing there by the bamboo, looking at him, imploring him with her eyes to come with her.

What the hell? thought Harry. If Charlie's around, then Charlie's gonna get me sooner or later, no matter *what* I do. Besides, maybe she's on the level. Maybe she'll show me what she did with my gear.

"Okay," he sighed. "Let's go."

The sopping ground squished under his feet and green tendrils brushed his face as he followed her through the unpleasant terrain that seemed to Harry to combine the worst features of both swamp and jungle. After they'd been walking for a minute or so, he saw to his astonishment that they were following a sort of path. Not much to it, but a path nonetheless.

Funny place for a path, Harry thought darkly. No villages or anything like that around here. The whole area belonged to Charlie. This path probably belonged to Charlie, too.

Mi's walk was both swift and graceful, and it seemed to Harry that she knew exactly where she was going. Walking behind her, he noticed that her sleeve was torn and that the bare flesh of her forearm seemed as smooth and soft as silk. She was a pretty girl, Harry decided, Vietnamese or not.

All the same, he should have thought twice about following her like this. She was taking him to Charlie . . . well, where else would she be taking him? If he was lucky, they'd kill him. Maybe they'd torture him first.

His mouth was dry.

It wasn't too late to turn back, to run back toward the river.

Mi stopped. So did Harry. She turned to him, said something he didn't understand, and pointed.

It was a rice paddy. Way out here in the middle of nowhere. Did Charlie grow his own rice, then?

Mi spoke again, quietly. There was a new timbre to her voice and her words hung in the air like little living things, and Harry wished that he understood what she was saying. She turned away, but not so quickly that he didn't see the glisten of tears in her eyes.

He was uneasy. It was only a rice paddy, nothing to

get excited about. It didn't make sense that she'd be crying over a rice paddy.

Skirting the paddy, they walked on.

Moments later, Harry smelled it. He stopped and stood where he was, and when Mi saw that he was no longer following her, she stopped too. She spoke to him, but he ignored her.

"What's that smell?"

He took a couple of deep breaths, trying to place the odor that seemed to pervade the jungle. A campfire? No, it was too strong. More like a burned-out field. Yeah, that's what it smelled like. A burned-out field.

Ten years ago, the woods above his folks' place had caught fire and burned down, and the day after the fire, when he and a couple of other boys had gone exploring in the ashes, it had smelled like this.

Mi went ahead, and Harry followed her. He found himself standing at the edge of a clearing. At least it looked like a clearing. Everything was burned away . . . and then it came to him, as suddenly and as completely and as horribly as a blow to the stomach. This had been a village. Those bits of charred wood, tipped and skewed, had been houses. The bloated piles of charred matter had been people.

There were flies, too. Here and there, a buzzing black, irridescent cloud hovered over a corpse that had not been totally consumed, stripping the last bits of flesh from the dead.

Mi fell to her knees alongside a shapeless mound of burned blackness, and the flies buzzed and rose in a cloud, and waited for her to be gone.

It was more than he could comprehend. Things like this weren't supposed to happen. It must have been an accident, a horrible accident. But even then, Harry knew that it hadn't been an accident, that this village had been destroyed as coldly and as completely as . . . what?

Again, his mind refused to put words to it.

Mi was on her feet now, moving slowly from corpse to corpse—she knows who they are, Harry thought in horror—saying a few words over each one. Ton Nam. Bich Ti. Hung Ba. She was saying their names, their *names* for God's sake! They'd been people, living breathing people. Her family. Her friends. Her village.

Mi stood erect in the midst of the blackened rubble. She looked up, and Harry followed her gaze. The sky was blue and serene, impossibly blue. Like the sky on a picture postcard.

She didn't say anything. She didn't have to. Harry knew what she was telling him.

"I'm . . . sorry." His voice stammered and struggled and gave up. He was sorry. It seemed a ridiculous, pathetic thing to say, and he was glad that she could not understand him. How do you apologize for a whole village full of people burned alive, burned to death? What kind of words do you use? Are there any words at all?

He stood there, shamed to silence. It was all that he could do—to stand where he was standing, and to look upon the grotesquely blackened remains of everything that Mi must have known and loved, and to remain silent.

A slight breeze wisped across the clearing, ruffling the black ashes. It wasn't decent. Dead people ought to be buried. He looked down, and then he saw it, so close to his foot that he might have kicked it.

A child. At least, it had been a child. It was small, and it had been burned through right down to its bones, but you could see that it had only been a little child, you could see its skull, not even as big as a softball . . .

The flies buzzed in the hot sunlight. And in the jungle, birds called back and forth.

God! thought Harry.

It was as close as he had ever come to praying.

# SIX

They were back at the river. Back where we started, Mi thought wearily. Haa-lee had wandered off by himself, and now he was sitting on a rock at the water's edge, doing something with several lengths of vine.

The baby slept at the foot of an areca palm. Mi and Ton were alone.

"You took him to our village." Ton's eyes blazed hurt and betrayal.

Mi nodded.

"But why?"

"I wanted him to understand."

"To understand what? To understand why we hate him?"

"I don't hate him, Ton."

"Well I do."

Ton was a child. He knew nothing of the world, despite all his brave bluster. Nothing. She'd been foolish to suppose that Ton would share the burden of responsibility. Whatever decisions would be made, she would have to make them alone.

"What did he do?" asked Ton. "Did he say anything?"

"Something in his own language. I don't know what it meant."

"And that's all? Nothing else happened?"

"Yes, that's all."

"You shouldn't have done it," Ton said then.

"I did it because I had to. And I don't want to talk about it, Ton. It's done and it's finished and I don't want to talk about it."

There were things that a child simply could not understand, and this was one of them. She had needed to know whether or not she could trust Haa-lee, really trust him. So she'd brought him to see the village, and she'd spoken of what had happened as if he was Vietnamese and could understand her words, and all the while she watched him, watched his face.

"He's going to help us," she said quietly.

"Help us? Why should he help us? He killed our mother, he burned our village—don't you think he's helped us enough?" Ton asked scornfully.

"Oh, be quiet."

Ton gave her a sullen, suspicious look. "You didn't tell me everything that happened, did you?"

"I've told you everything you need to know." But Ton was right. Something *had* happened—something wordless—between them. Somehow, her relationship with Haa-lee had changed, although she didn't quite know how . . . or even why.

She could not yet explain it to herself, this new feeling that she had. Certainly, she could not explain it to Ton.

"You treat me like a child," he complained.

"Stop acting like one, and I'll stop treating you like one."

He took a step backward, as if she'd struck him. His face was flushed with anger, and she was sorry that she'd been so flippant. But really, he was so . . .

"They're very wealthy, the American soldiers." A new and unpleasant tone had crept into Ton's voice. "Is that what you want? Is that why you're being so nice to him? Do you hope he'll marry you, and make you rich?"

"How dare you . . ."

"How dare *you!*" Ton flung back at her. "He is our enemy. And now, all of a sudden, you make a friend of him. Why? Why should he help us? He is an American and we are Vietnamese. We are at war. Have you fallen in love with him, then?"

He is too young to know what he is saying, Mi told herself. This is more of Hung Ba's poison.

She did not try to defend herself. No matter what she said, it would not convince him and would only make things worse. Deliberately, she gazed past him at the matted green of the jungle, and the silence between them grew and grew.

"Mi . . ."

After all, he was only a child. No matter what he said, no matter what he thought, he was nine years old and he was a child. She would have to be patient. But when she turned to speak to him, resentment flared within her like a dying ember and the comforting, forgiving words stuck in her throat and refused to come. So she remained silent, and simply looked at him and waited to see what he would do.

75

"I didn't mean it," Ton said uneasily, his eyes scanning her face for a sign of what she was thinking. "I didn't mean what I said, Mi. Really, I didn't."

"Then why did you say it?"

He hung his head.

"We're lucky to be alive, don't you know that? Out of the whole village . . ." she hesitated. She didn't want to talk about the village; she didn't even want to think about it. "I'm doing my best, Ton. Can't you understand that?"

He nodded, wordlessly.

"Why won't you help me, then? Why do you fight me? Why do you try to hurt me? Why do you sulk and complain and make things even worse than they are?"

"I don't know," Ton replied miserably to everything. "It's just that you . . ."

"It's just that I *what?*"

He hesitated. "You're different. You're not the way you used to be, not at all. You don't even talk the way you used to talk. You—you act like Mama. But you're not Mama!" insisted Ton vehemently. "You're not! And it's no good pretending you are, either!"

"Is that what you think?" She was suddenly tired, so tired that she wanted to cry. "Is that really what you think I'm doing? Pretending that I'm Mama?"

"You're different. That's all. You're just different."

She couldn't reach him. Not with words, at any rate. Besides, perhaps he was right. Perhaps she *was* different. Certainly, she didn't feel as if she was the same person she'd been yesterday morning, or even last night.

"We're both tired," she said at last. "But we shouldn't argue like this. Really, we shouldn't."

"Well, I said I was sorry."

"I'm sorry too," said Mi.

There was a short, uncomfortable silence.

"I'm going to get a drink of water," Ton said then. "Do you want one?"

She shook her head, but she smiled too, so that he'd know she was no longer angry.

It was already past noon. A whole day wasted! Ton went off toward the river, and Mi sighed, pushed her hair back from her damp forehead, and then went to see about the little ones.

Worn out by all that had happened to her, Bong had finally gone to sleep. Her little face was still swollen from crying, but her breathing was slow and even, and her slumber seemed peaceful. Lying on her back with one arm flung out to the side, she looked even tinier and younger than she was.

Slowly, Mi looked around. To her back, the jungle loomed like a solid wall of green. A hundred paces ahead, the river surged brown and angry, rising with every hour that passed. This flat, damp strip of ground between the jungle and the river—this was all that was left to them. And in a day or so, even this would be gone.

Mi moved restlessly toward the water.

Small animals in traps must feel like this, she thought. Little fish caught in nets. Prisoners and slaves must feel like this. And nightingales, locked into cages and blinded with hot pokers so that they would sing more sweetly.

She stared and stared at the river, trying not to remember how the village had looked. Then she turned, and walked slowly back to where Bong was.

Bong was lucky. She was so young that she wouldn't remember much of this; she might not remember anything at all. Nor would the baby remember, Mi thought.

The baby wouldn't even remember Mama. The tears that she'd blinked back a moment ago swam in her eyes, and this time, they spilled out onto her cheeks, hot and salty. Somehow, it was the worst thing of all, that the baby wouldn't remember Mama.

Why had this happened to them? Why? Shuddering a little, Mi shut her eyes tight and pressed her knuckles against her eyelids, willing the tears to stop. She mustn't give in. Not yet. Not until they were all safe in Saigon, with Papa.

She knelt down to see if the baby was all right. Like Bong, he was asleep. There was nothing strange about that. The children always napped during the hottest part of the day. Everybody did. Even the *fonctionnaires* in the city left their offices at noon and did not return until mid-afternoon. It was too hot for a sensible person to do anything else.

All the same, she was concerned about the baby. He ought to have been awake and screaming with hunger. He hadn't had anything to eat or drink since last night. She tickled his cheek with her fingertip, but he didn't stir.

Mi knelt there for a long time, gazing at him.

Ton had gotten his drink of water, and now he was sitting in the shade of an areca palm, his arms wrapped around his knees, watching Haa-lee. It was time that she and Ton became friends again. Mi went and sat down beside him.

Haa-lee was standing in the river, bare-headed and up to his waist in water. "What is he doing now?" Mi asked.

"He's fishing."

"Fishing? With what?"

"He's got a net."

"But where did he get it?"

"He made it out of vines."

"Out of *vines?* Ton, are you sure?"

"I saw him."

Mi waited, but Ton didn't add anything more. He just sat there like a lump of clay and stared at the river.

"Do you think he'll catch anything?" she asked at last.

Ton shrugged. "He might catch a crayfish, or something like that. But what difference does it make? Even if he does catch something that's big enough to eat, we won't be able to cook it because we don't have any matches. We'll have to eat it raw." And he spat, contemptuously.

Mi started to scold him, then thought better of it, and held her tongue. She could not talk Ton out of his hatred for Haa-lee, and she knew it. One might just as well try to talk the sun out of the sky.

They sat side by side, silent, each thinking his own thoughts.

Suddenly, Haa-lee lost his footing and sprawled headlong into the river, splashing and thrashing and tangling himself in his net. Ton laughed, and it was all that Mi could do not to laugh too.

Ton continued to laugh, even after Haa-lee had regained his balance.

"That's enough," Mi said uncomfortably.

To her amazement, Ton leaped to his feet. "You always take his side!" he cried, almost in tears. "You don't care about me, or Bong, or anybody but him . . ." Choking on his sobs, he raced blindly into the jungle.

Mi let him go. He'd feel better after he'd had a good cry . . .

She closed her eyes. What would become of them now? she wondered. They couldn't stay here. There was no food, no shelter. The river was rising. And suppose the American bombers came back?

Haa-lee. Oh, how she wished she could talk to him, really talk to him. The little book that he carried, the book of Vietnamese phrases, was almost worse than nothing at all. It was full of silly commonplaces. The things that she would have liked to ask him—"Do you have a wife?" and "Why are you a soldier?" and "How old are you?"—these things did not appear in Haa-lee's book.

Mi opened her eyes. Haa-lee's makeshift net had begun to come apart, and he'd waded ashore and was kneeling in the grass a few feet from where she sat, trying to knot the ends of the vines. His hands were quick and deft, as if he'd done this kind of thing before. That was strange, too. He knew how to make a fishing-net out of vines—something that Mi would have thought impossible—and yet, he did not know how to use it.

The net repaired, Haa-lee stood up. He was barefoot, and the skin of his feet and ankles looked very white against the brown grass. Such long toes! Mi stared, not able to help it. Did all Americans have such long toes?

It was then that Mi saw his feet were bleeding. She frowned. Had he been hurt?

As if he could feel her eyes upon him, Haa-lee turned and looked back at her. Embarrassed, Mi lowered her eyes. She made a gesture toward his feet.

Laughing, Haa-lee said something in that harsh, unmanageable language of his and went back to his fishing.

But what could have happened to his feet? Mi pondered it curiously. Such white, tender feet! Like a small child's feet, really. Perhaps he'd cut them on the rocky river bottom. No wonder the Americans wear such thick, heavy boots, Mi thought, if their feet are as delicate as that. And Haa-lee had lost his boots, lost them in the river.

She would make some sandals for him. There were plenty of reeds here along the river. She would make sandals for all of them, for herself and for Bong, even a pair for Ton, if there was time. Mi smiled. Suddenly, there was so much time . . .

The baby cried out then and Mi leaped up and ran to him, forgetting Haa-lee, forgetting the sandals she was going to make, forgetting everything in the apprehension that engulfed her. It was only then that she realized how frightened she really was, how concerned.

But what am I afraid of? she demanded. What do I think is wrong with him? What do I think is going to happen?

There was only that one cry. By the time that Mi reached down and picked him up, the baby had gone back to sleep.

She held him, cradling him close against her body. A little bit of fever. Not very much. Not enough to worry about. Yet she didn't want to put him down. Still holding him, she returned to her seat at the base of the tree.

She watched as Haa-lee continued to cast his net, again and again. He seemed to have become more adept, more sure of himself. He'd taken off his shirt, and the strong muscles of his back rippled in the hot sunshine, tan and smooth. He was much taller and much heavier than a Vietnamese would be. Mi giggled, thinking of some of the whispered stories that she'd heard about Vietnamese girls who'd married American men. Then, remembering what Ton had said, she felt her face go hot with embarrassment.

Still, Haa-lee amazed her. She'd had certain ideas

about what an American was like—nearly everybody did these days—and Haa-lee was nothing at all like what she would have expected him to be. He was . . . good. Mi thought of a proverb: You do not use good iron to make nails, nor a good man to make a soldier. It was an Eastern proverb, and it was true in the East. But perhaps in America, it wasn't true.

Certainly, Haa-lee was a good man. And perhaps a good soldier, too.

The baby lay motionless in her arms, snoring a little, hot and heavy as a poultice. Mi laid him down upon a soft hummock of grass. She was hot and uncomfortable. She felt dirty. She would have liked to take off her shift and bathe in the river.

Again, she blushed.

Ton. She would have to try to be more patient with him. Poor Ton. He was too young to understand that what happened wasn't Haa-lee's fault.

It was so quiet, here by the river. So peaceful. And yet yesterday . . .

Mi shut her eyes, and vowed that she would not think of what had happened yesterday. She would think of tomorrow, and the day after tomorrow. She would think of Papa, in Saigon.

Yawning a little and rubbing at her eyes as if she were a child, Mi wandered down to the river's edge and sat on a flat rock that jutted out over the water. Haa-lee was so engrossed with casting his net that he didn't even look up. Dabbling her bare feet in the water, Mi splashed them a little, wanting him to notice her.

Did he think she was pretty? Probably not, Mi thought sadly. She sat quietly, her feet tucked under her, watching him as he cast his net again and again into the turbulent, gray waters.

The long day faded slowly into dusk.

Haa-lee managed to catch five fish—they were small, but at least they weren't crayfish—and Mi set to work cleaning them. She was strangely content to kneel there, cleaning the fish that he'd caught with the little knife that he'd taught her how to use. It was like being part of a family again. The knife itself amazed her. It was as light and tiny as a toy, yet it was even more efficient than the thick, fire-blackened cleaver that Mama had always used for such tasks.

It was almost dark by the time Ton came back. He'd brought a few bananas with him, and a small coconut. He offered no excuse for having stayed away so long, and Mi didn't ask him for one.

The baby slept on peacefully, but Bong woke up and cried for water. Mi brought it to her in a leaf that she'd folded into a cone-shaped cup, and Bong drank thirstily.

"My leg hurts."

"I know," sympathized Mi. "You've got to lie very still, and then it won't hurt as much. Here, let me help you sit up. We'll prop you up against this big rock, like this. Now isn't that better?"

Bong looked curiously around the clearing. "Are we going to build a house of bamboo and stay here forever and ever?"

"Would you like that?"

The little girl thought for a moment, and then shook her head. "I think I'd like to go home."

"We can't go home. But we're going to Saigon instead!" Mi continued hurriedly. "It's the biggest city in Vietnam, and it's full of big, tall buildings and parks and wonderful shops and a zoo and a whole street full of flower stalls . . ."

"But we didn't say good-bye to Mama."

"Mama is dead, Bong."

"I know. And she's gone away to live in the Jade Emperor's court, hasn't she? But I wish I could have kissed her good-bye," Bong added, wistfully.

Mi turned away, unable to speak.

"Are you crying because you miss Mama?"

"I'm not crying at all. I've . . . I've just got something in my eye. There, it's out now, see?" Somehow, she managed to smile. Bong smiled too. "I've got to go and see to Little Brother. I'll tell Ton to come and sit with you. Maybe you can persuade him to tell you a story."

The baby was lying so quietly that Mi thought he was still asleep . . . but then she saw that his eyes were open, and bright with fever.

This was what she had feared.

Picking him up, she held him close against her shoulder and walked down to the river's edge. He was listless in her arms, and his skin was hot and dry. Mi knelt with him, and splashed cool water onto his face and wrists and little ankles. She remembered that only three weeks ago she'd watched Truong Li Li do the same thing for her own baby, and the Truong baby had died only hours later.

Mi shivered, and tried to force the thought from her mind.

The Truong baby's death had made everyone in the village apprehensive, not because a child had died—that was sad, but it was no more unusual for a less-than-one-year-old baby to die than it was for a woman to die in childbirth—but rather, because the Truong baby's death had come so quickly, so quietly, so peculiarly.

In the morning, Truong Li Li's baby had refused the breast. By afternoon there was fever, but no one thought anything of that. Most babies had a fever at one time

84

or another, and most got over it. But the next morning, Truong Li Li's anguished wails awakened half the village . . .

Mi drew a slow, steadying breath. I'm getting to be as bad as Ton, she thought. Making everything into a drama or a disaster.

Still carrying the baby, she went to see what Haa-lee was doing. Ton hadn't managed to steal all of his matches after all, she observed, and it was a good thing he hadn't. The first little flames of a cooking fire flickered from the tiny hearth Haa-lee had built in the center of the clearing, and Mi smiled and thought how good the fish would taste.

She wandered back to the river. The last glimmers of light made it look thick and smooth as oil. The water seemed to be higher now than it had been earlier this afternoon. That rock, for instance, the rounded, grayish one just a meter or so from where she was standing. Hadn't it jutted out above the surface of the water? She was sure that it had. Now it was completely submerged, with only a fringe of froth to trace the outline of where it had been.

We must leave tomorrow, thought Mi. No matter what happens.

Now that the sun was gone, the breeze had a chilling bite to it and Mi turned back to the clearing and to Haa-lee's cheerfully blazing fire. She paused a few steps away from where he sat, and looked at him. What did he think of all of this? she wondered. How did he feel? His face, highlighted now by the orange glow of the fire, was so unlike a Vietnamese face that it was difficult for Mi to attribute any emotions whatsoever to it. So pale! And the nose was so large!

How strange and awkward it would be, Mi thought,

to have such a big nose. Americans were really quite funny-looking. Perhaps that was why they were so aggressive—perhaps they had to be aggressive, so that other people wouldn't laugh at them.

Sensing her eyes upon him, Haa-lee turned. Mi lowered her own eyes hurriedly, wondering what he must think of her. Even a tea-girl wouldn't stare and stare as she had been doing. All the same, she'd heard that American women were much more forward than other women, and that American men liked it. It was whispered that in the United States, men and women allowed their hands and bodies to touch in public, and made a practice of kissing one another upon the mouth. But Mi didn't believe *that* . . . it was too disgusting, even for Americans.

Ton was still talking to Bong, but he'd begun to scrape the meat out of his coconut. Mi put the baby down and set to work on the fish, wrapping each one in a banana leaf and then setting it among the smoldering coals. It was quite dark by now, and chilly. Haa-lee helped Mi to move Bong closer to the fire. His hands were deft and gentle.

They ate hungrily, not even talking between mouthfuls. Even Bong—who usually didn't like fleshy fish unless it was doused in *muoc mam,* fish sauce—finished everything that was put before her. Mi took this to mean that her leg was healing properly, without infection, and she was relieved.

As soon as she'd eaten her own dinner, Mi took the baby onto her lap and coaxed him with bits of banana and sips of the broth that she'd cooked in the coconut shell. It was no use. Weak and listless as he was, he wouldn't eat.

"Just like the Truong baby," muttered Ton.

"Hush!" hissed Mi. "Do you want to frighten Bong?"
There was a short silence.

"He likes sweet things," Ton said then. "There's some sugar cane growing wild just down the river. Do you want me to go and get some of it for him?"

Mi shook her head. "He's not hungry. All babies get like this once in a while. It's nothing to worry about."

Ton didn't believe a word of it, she could see that. But mercifully, for Bong's sake, he held his tongue.

"What are you going to do?" asked Ton, after another silence.

"We'll see how he is tomorrow."

"And if he's no better?"

"He'll be better, you'll see."

But all the same, she was afraid.

Warmed by the fire and the food, Bong yawned sleepily. Mi helped her lie down, made her comfortable. In a moment, she was asleep. Ton stretched, and leaned back against one of the trees, and stared moodily into the flickering embers.

Now that the breeze had died down, the night was soft and warm and rhythmic with the hum of insects and the almost inaudible scurry of night creatures. Later, there would be a moon. It was hard to believe that yesterday and today had really happened, that their village no longer lay where it had always been, slumbering behind the banana trees and the bamboo.

Haa-lee said something, something soft and quiet. Mi looked at him, but it was so dark that she could see nothing of his face save the whitish gleam of his teeth.

"Why does he bother to talk? He knows we can't understand him and he knows that he can't understand us."

"Perhaps he's lonely," replied Mi.

"Soldiers don't get lonely."

"How do you know? You've never been a soldier."

"I've practiced being a soldier," Ton said stoutly. "And that's the same thing."

"You've played at being a soldier. And that's not the same thing at all."

"It just so happens . . ."

"Oh, Ton, let's not argue."

He grumbled, then lapsed into silence.

The baby lay quietly in her lap. In the darkness, Mi could not tell whether or not he was asleep, but his breathing was slow and regular, and his forehead was not quite so hot as it had been a few hours earlier.

Making herself as comfortable as she could, Mi looked sleepily at the fire. It had almost burned itself out by now; it was little more than a mound of glowing embers and an occasional tongue of flame. Above their heads, the sky was jeweled with stars . . . the Silver River, Mi thought drowsily, remembering the fairy tales of her childhood. The Silver River and the Jade Emperor's fairy court . . .

She slept.

Her first thought was that she'd had a bad dream. She turned slightly, as she would have turned upon her own sleeping-mat, and then she remembered. She remembered everything, despairingly. But what was it that had awakened her? The sky was gray and damp, and a pre-dawn mist hung like an opaque veil over the whole of the clearing.

The baby. He was gone. Her arms were cold and empty.

Terror gripped her. She groped on the ground in front of her, hardly daring to think.

8 8

"Mi, is that you?"

"The baby . . . "

"I've got him," Ton said quickly. "But you'd better come here."

On her hands and knees, Mi crept toward the sound of his voice. He was squatting alongside the cold ash remnants of last night's fire, holding the baby gingerly out in front of him. As if he'd never held a baby before, Mi thought angrily.

"Here," she said impatiently. "Give him to me before you drop him."

"Be careful. He might . . . "

And then she saw for herself, and gasped, and for a long moment she simply knelt there on the cold ground, holding the baby in her own arms and staring down at him as if by simply looking at him, she could change him back to what he'd been a few short hours ago.

"But what happened?"

"I don't know," said Ton miserably.

The baby was still, as still as death itself. His limbs were cold and stiff, and his eyes had rolled up and back into his head so that only the whites were visible. A trickle of saliva drooled horribly from his open, flaccid mouth. Mi's fingers groped frantically across his chest, then found the fluttering heart-beat that told her that he was still alive, that no matter what had happened, it was still not too late.

"Tell me what happened. Tell me quickly."

"He . . . he started to cry. Not loudly. Just a little bit. You were sleeping, so I went and picked him up. I thought he might be hungry or thirsty, or something like that. I didn't do anything to him, though. All I did was pick him up."

"Yes, but what happened?"

"It was so quick. And I didn't know what to do. He threw his head back, like this, and he made a funny noise in his throat. It sounded like he was choking on something, and I didn't know what to do. And then his legs got stiff, and his arms, and then—it stopped."

"Why didn't you wake me?"

"I was going to, but I was afraid that I'd wake up Bong, and I was afraid to move him, too. I thought maybe if I just sat and held him for a while, maybe he'd be all right. But . . . "

"How long?" interrupted Mi. "How long has he been like this?"

"Not long. Just a couple of minutes."

Was this what had happened to Truong Li Li's baby? A strange, sudden sickness, a sickness that resembled madness. No wonder Truong Li Li had not wanted to talk about it afterwards!

Suddenly, Haa-lee appeared behind her, speaking in whispers, asking questions that Mi could neither answer nor understand. But there was no misunderstanding the concern and compassion in his eyes, and Mi spoke to him exactly as she would have spoken to one of her own family. "We don't know what the matter is. But he's sick, terribly sick."

Nodding as if he'd understood every word she'd said, Haa-lee squatted down and placed his thumb and forefinger about the baby's tiny wrist.

"What's he doing?" Ton asked suspiciously.

"I don't know."

Shaking his head slightly, Haa-lee let the baby's hand drop.

It was lighter now, and warmer. Soon the sun would rise. Through the thinning mists, Mi could see that the eastern sky beyond the river was already suffused with rosy color.

"A doctor," she murmured. "We've got to get him to a doctor."

Ton gave her an anguished look. "But there aren't any doctors! How can we?"

"There's a doctor in Vinh Luc. He comes to the convent school every month. He might be there now, and even if he isn't, there'll be other people there, other women. Surely someone will know what to do."

"But there's nothing left of Vinh Luc. They bombed it. Don't you remember?"

She'd forgotten. Vinh Luc was gone. There would be no doctor, no help, nothing at all in Vinh Luc. Still holding the baby, she shut her eyes. It would have been better if we'd died, she thought, all of us, in the village with Mama.

Why do we struggle? she wondered hopelessly. What difference does it make, whether we die together or whether we die one by one? It would be better to die now, to die quickly, to die together. Because no matter what we do, we're going to die. Look at us! Just look at us! As helpless as chickens or pigs, bound and crated and on the way to market.

Helpless, helpless . . .

It was then that Haa-lee reached out and took her hand, and held it in his own.

Mi looked up. She found that she was looking into Haa-lee's eyes, gazing into them.

*He cares about us. He cares about me. He wants to help.*

It was like reading words on a printed page.

His fingers gripped hers for a second longer—how

strong he must be, to have so much strength in his fingers—and then his hand dropped to his side.

Ton was gaping, too astonished to speak.

Only the coarsest and most indelicate Saigon prostitutes allowed themselves to be thus touched by a man who was not kin.

As for Mi, she knew what she must do.

"Go and wake Bong," she told Ton. "Be gentle. If she asks about the baby, tell her that he's still asleep."

Ton didn't move.

"Go on, do what I say! Every minute counts!"

"But—but what are we going to do?"

"We're going to find a doctor. If we have to go all the way to Saigon, then we'll go to Saigon. But we're not going to let him die, do you understand? We're not going to let him die!"

"But . . ."

"Just do what I tell you to do!"

Ton stared, then ran to wake Bong.

Mi turned to Haa-lee. "You'll help us, won't you? You've got to help us. We can't manage alone. Not now, not with Bong hurt. Here, watch me." She knelt beside him, groped for a stick, and brushed hastily at the bare ground, clearing a place so that she could draw. "I'm drawing a map, do you see?"

The tip of the stick moved quickly and Haa-lee leaned closer, watching carefully.

"There, it's done. Now, we're here." She placed the tip of her stick upon the X she'd drawn to mark their location. "Vinh Luc is here, but the town's gone. There's a bridge though, here. And then as soon as we get across the bridge, here's the road." She moved her makeshift pointer along the map slowly, letting Haa-lee follow it with his eyes. "This is Saigon, up here. But we probably won't have to go as far as that. I hope we won't. But I don't know." She looked up at him. "Do you understand? Will you help us?"

Their eyes met over the map and Haa-lee nodded.

He understood.

They left moments later, just as the sun burst from the blood-pink eastern horizon.

Ton walked ahead, carrying a stick with which he beat at the tall grasses, scaring the snakes that had sought refuge from the rising waters. Mi followed several paces behind, holding the baby so that his head rested easily against her shoulder. Haa-lee, who carried Bong as easily as if she weighed nothing and as gently as if she were his own, brought up the rear. Slowly, they moved along the edge of the river toward Vinh Luc; or at least, Mi thought, toward the place where Vinh Luc had once been.

Urgency throbbed in her blood like a fever. Faster! she wanted to cry. We've got to go faster!

The sun climbed slowly up the blue-sided bowl of the sky, mocking death. Birds sang. The countryside fell away on either side, green and lovely. A cooling breeze wafted off the river, adding to the cruel, uncaring beauty of the day. Mi hated it for being so beautiful, so indifferent.

Toward noon, they stopped to rest. Haa-lee sat Bong down on the grass, while Ton went to fetch her a drink of water. Lack of food had made Mi dizzy, and a little light-headed. She settled herself on a flat rock apart from the others, and gazed sadly down at the baby's still, expressionless face. Was he really going to die? Was there no way to save him?

The blind need to *do* something gripped her . . . yet

what was there to do? The question beat savagely through her thoughts, again and again, numbing her. She could feel him slipping farther and farther away from her, she could feel him growing weaker and weaker . . . but what could she do?

He was dying. He was so young that he had not even been given a name, and yet he was dying.

Haa-lee came toward her, then hesitated. She nodded to him, so that he came and sat beside her. It made her feel better to have him near, and she no longer cared what Ton thought or didn't think.

Haa-lee reached out, and Mi, without even thinking about it, gave the baby into his arms. He looked at the child carefully, the way a doctor might look at a patient. Did he perhaps know something of medicine? Americans were said to be very intelligent. Mi searched his strange, grave face for some sign of hope or encouragement, but found only a sadness that seemed to match her own.

"It's no good," she said quietly, when he'd placed the baby back in her arms. "It's just no good. He's asleep, and he won't wake up. I don't think he'll ever wake up again. And yet, I keep thinking that maybe he will. I keep hoping. He was such a good baby, you know. He was, he really was."

It helped to talk. Even though Haa-lee couldn't understand what she was saying, it helped.

"He's going to die. He's going to die just the same way that Truong Li Li's baby died. She's dead too, now. Truong Li Li, I mean. She and her baby and her two little girls, all dead."

Haa-lee's eyes never left her face. Could he understand any of the things she was saying? Of course he couldn't understand. He was an American, and he could not speak Vietnamese. Was there a word for "death" in his little book? wondered Mi.

For a moment, she hated him.

The moment passed. It wasn't his fault, after all. And he was trying to help.

If only Vinh Luc hadn't been destroyed, mused Mi, there still might have been a chance. Not a very big chance, but a chance. A doctor might have known what to do. But there wouldn't be a doctor in Vinh Luc. Not now. Not ever again.

Mi had never actually been inside Vinh Luc's little convent school, but she'd often stood on the roadway and looked at it, wondering at the white-robed women who sometimes appeared in the courtyards. During the past few years, the school had been pressed into service as a hospital as well, and every fortnight an old Chinese doctor came all the way from the Catholic mission in Cai Nuoc . . . *Cai Nuoc.*

"The mission! There's a doctor at the mission!"

Haa-lee stared at her, worried. Did he think she'd gone mad?

"There's a Catholic mission in Cai Nuoc. And they've got a doctor, a Chinese doctor. Nguyen Tai Son went to him when her hands began to grow stiff, and he gave her medicine, and in three days she was able to go out into the paddies and plant rice. Nguyen Tai Son was a Catholic, and that's why she went to Cai Nuoc."

"What are you talking about?" Ton had been standing behind her, eavesdropping. "What about Cai Nuoc?"

"The doctor, the Chinese doctor! The one that Nguyen Tai Son went to, remember? And Cai Nuoc's not far from here. All we've got to do is cross the bridge and then cut inland . . ."

"We can't go to Cai Nuoc," interrupted Ton.

Mi stared at him, unable to believe her own ears. "What do you mean? Of course we can go to Cai Nuoc! And . . . "

"No, we can't. Not with *him,* anyway."

"What are you talking about?"

Ton hesitated, looking to the right and then to the left, as if he thought the impenetrable bamboo thickets concealed a host of spies. Mi could have shaken him.

"Are you going to tell me what you're talking about, or aren't you?"

"It's a secret."

"Ton, I'm warning you . . . "

Mi waited, pale with anger.

"It's a supply center for the nationalists," said Ton, pitching his voice low and speaking so fast that Mi could barely understand him. "There's not a hut or a chicken coop or a pig run in the whole town that doesn't have grain stored underneath. And not just grain, either!" A note of pride crept into Ton's voice. "Guns, ammunition, medicines, grenades, food, maps, radios—everything we need to slaughter them."

Oh, what nonsense! But she forced herself to be patient. "I don't care about your nationalists! All I care about is this baby, and this baby will die if I don't get him to a doctor. Can't you get that through your head? I don't care about the nationalists, and I don't care about their secrets. It's got nothing to do with me."

"It's got plenty to do with *him,* though." Ton jerked his head toward Haa-lee. "They've got look-outs, all along the road. They'd take one look at us—and at him—and they'd shoot us down before we even got as far as the first market."

"But we could explain . . . "

"They wouldn't give us a chance. And even if they

did, how *would* you explain? What would you say? That this Haa-lee—this American soldier—is our friend? Is that what you'd say? Or perhaps you'd say that he was our prisoner?"

Mi hesitated. It might be that this was one more of Hung Ba's outrageous half-truths. Rumors like this one flew about the countryside like crows, and provincial governments changed so frequently that nobody bothered to keep track of them.

Bowing her head, she gazed at the baby who lay so quietly in her arms. "If we don't get him to a doctor, he'll die."

"Besides, the doctor might not even be there. He might be dead. Or in prison. Nobody trusts the Catholics anymore, and nobody ever trusted the Chinese to begin with . . . "

"We're going to Cai Nuoc."

"We can't."

"We can, and we will."

"And when they shoot us?"

"They won't shoot us. When we're still ten or fifteen kilometers away from Cai Nuoc, Haa-lee and I will take Bong and hide in one of the bamboo thickets along the canal. You will continue along the road with Little Brother. A boy carrying a sick baby—who would have the heart to question you? Even an American soldier would let you pass."

Ton gnawed at his lower lip. "What about you? If they catch you, they'll kill you."

"*I'm* not afraid."

Ton bridled. "And you think I am?"

Mi said nothing.

"All right, then. Cai Nuoc. If you think you can manage your American," added Ton.

It was agreed, then.

"You're going to get well," Mi whispered to the baby, pressing him close to her. "We're going to take you to the Chinese doctor in Cai Nuoc, and he's going to make you well."

It was not to be.

The baby died in her arms—quietly, without even opening his eyes for a last look—just as they reached the heap of charred rubbish that was all that remained of Vinh Luc.

# SEVEN

Harry stood at the edge of the river, uneasy, wondering what was going to happen. He'd put Bong down, and now his hands hung at his sides, feeling big and empty and awkward.

He didn't know where they were, except that it looked as if it might have been some kind of settlement before it'd been bombed out. Now it was just a pile of junk, scraps of twisted tin and hunks of timber all over the place, and the jungle already starting to grow back over everything.

Squinting against the glare, he let his eyes move slowly across the surging river as he gauged the distance from here to the far bank. Not too bad, unless the water was deeper than it looked. And Cai Nuoc was over there someplace. Mi had said so. He hadn't realized that they were this close to Cai Nuoc.

He glanced at Mi. She stood quietly, her face as blank and as expressionless as the sun-blasted sky. She was still holding the baby. She was holding it as if it were alive. But it wasn't alive, and she shouldn't be holding it like that. It gave him the creeps, the way she was holding that baby.

There was a stale, sour taste in his mouth. He swallowed, licked his lips, swallowed again.

Somebody ought to do something. They couldn't stand here like this forever, could they? Somebody ought to take the baby away from Mi, take it away and bury it. Yeah. Somebody ought to do that, and do it fast.

No one moved. Not even Bong, whose unblinking eyes reminded Harry of a doll's eyes, shiny black buttons that saw everything and saw nothing.

Mi cleared her throat then, and started to say something to Ton. But after only a couple of words, her voice trembled and broke. And now, the silence was unbearable.

You'd think that they'd cry or something. White people would have cried. Or cursed. Or said something. But not these people, not the Vietnamese. It puzzled him, the way these people hid their feelings. It wasn't natural.

"Look, if there's anything you want me to do . . . "

He stopped, embarrassed. She couldn't understand anything he said, and besides, there was nothing he *could* do. There was nothing anyone could do now. Dead. The baby was dead.

Ton turned, and walked slowly back toward the thick, green tangle of undergrowth and banana and bamboo that walled the river. Harry frowned. Dead baby or no dead baby, he was going to keep an eye on Ton. No telling what the little bastard might do. Without looking back, Ton dropped to his knees and began to grub around in the dirt.

"What's he doing? What's he up to?"

But he could already see what Ton was doing. Harry felt his own face go hot with shame. Ton was digging a grave.

"Here, let me give you a hand."

Turning, Ton gave him a swift, malevolent look that stopped him in his tracks.

"All right, I'm sorry. I just wanted to help."

But Ton was already on his feet, jabbering furiously at Mi. She stood there without saying a word, holding the baby and letting Ton talk just the way you'd let a little wind-up toy run down.

Ton finally went back to work.

"You know what he needs? He needs a good swift kick, right where it'd do the most good. He shouldn't talk to you like that. He ought to learn some manners, some respect. You know what I mean?"

Mi gave him a long, thoughtful look, and then she turned her back on him.

Ton laughed, a short, savage bark of a laugh.

Jesus Christ! She didn't have to act like that, did she? It wasn't his fault that the baby had died.

Ton shouted something.

"Go to hell."

He walked away, fast. Here was the river. For two cents, he'd dive in and swim across and leave the three of them here to do anything they wanted to do. Leave them just the way he'd found them. And why not? They needed him, but he sure as hell didn't need them. Besides, if they were anywhere near Cai Nuoc . . .

"Haa-lee."

To hell with her.

*"Haa-lee."*

He turned around slowly. Mi was looking at him, her lips slightly parted, her eyes like luminous brown lights in her face.

He felt sorry for her, and ashamed of himself. What did he expect, anyway? She was just a kid, a worn-out, scared, unhappy kid. The past couple of days had been pretty grim for her, and the future . . . well, what kind of future *could* she have?

And the baby dying, on top of everything else . . . it was a damn shame about the baby.

"Look, I'm sorry. I didn't mean it. I'm not going anyplace, okay?"

She just kept looking at him, scared.

If she'd been a little kid, he'd have smiled at her and given her a piece of candy. Like a peace offering. But she wasn't a little kid. And besides, he didn't have any candy.

Did she really think he'd walk away and leave her? After all that they'd been through together, did she really think he'd go and do a lousy thing like that? She didn't know him very well, if she thought he'd pull a stunt like that . . .

Of course she didn't know him. How could she?

All Americans are bastards, that's probably what she was thinking. And after having seen what a squadron of B-52s had done to her village, Harry couldn't blame her for thinking that. But all the same . . .

She hadn't moved. She was still standing there, looking at him. But her face had changed. Now it was taut with pain, and her eyes were bright, too bright, brimming with unshed tears. It hurt him to see her like this. It wasn't right, damn it. It just wasn't right.

Ton's sharp voice shattered the silence. Whatever it was he said, it hit Mi and it hit her hard. Her face went chalky-pale, and she seemed to stagger. For a moment, Harry thought she was going to collapse right there on the spot, baby and all. But she didn't collapse. With a visible effort, she stood straight and then turned away from Harry to walk back to where Ton was standing and waiting for her.

They were arguing about something. Harry couldn't understand what they were saying, but they both looked upset and their voices, though not loud, not even shrill, were tense. Whatever it was, it looked like Ton was getting the best of it.

The argument—if that was what it had been—ended as abruptly as it had begun. Mi and Ton stood silent, side by side, gazing down at the grave.

Harry took a step back. He felt like an outsider. He *was* an outsider, and he knew it.

Bowing her head, Mi kissed the baby upon its forehead. Then, wrapping him for the last time in the uneven scrap of cloth that was to be his shroud, she placed the small, motionless bundle into Ton's arms. As she backed away, she stumbled a little bit and Harry saw that she was crying. Silently. But crying.

Ton hesitated. Then he knelt and laid the baby's body into the grave. And that was all. Rapidly, Ton's hands scooped the earth back into place, covering the baby's body, fashioning a raw mound that stood out cruelly against the jungle's blatant greenery. It was over.

Harry felt sick. He looked away.

It had all happened so fast, so damned fast. When he'd

found them, the baby had been fine, it hadn't been sick or hurt. And now it was dead. It got sick, and it died. No doctor. No medicine. Nothing. It just didn't seem right, that a baby could die like that.

It wasn't the first time that Harry had seen death, but it was the first time that he'd stopped to think what it meant, dying. To die. It meant that everything was over, everything was finished. And some day, it would happen to him . . .

Bong started to cry, very quietly. No one paid any attention to her, and after a moment or two, she stopped.

Ton said something to Mi and she nodded. He turned and ran into the jungle. This time, Harry let him go.

Now what? Mi had gone back to the little grave and she was kneeling there, her head bowed, her hands clasped in front of her. Maybe she was praying. Harry thought that she looked like a princess out of some childhood fairy tale, with her pale face and that long, black hair hanging like a silken curtain down her back.

Minutes passed, Harry didn't know how many. Mi hadn't moved, and Ton hadn't come back.

Then Mi turned and looked up at him.

"I wish it hadn't happened . . . "

What was the use of talking? She couldn't understand him, and even if she had understood him—even if she'd been an American—it wouldn't have made any difference, because the baby was dead. Words couldn't help, words couldn't bring him back. Not English words, and not Vietnamese words either.

She was still looking at him, waiting for something.

God! If only there was something he could say, something he could do.

She'd think that he didn't care. She'd think that just because she was Vietnamese, he didn't care. He couldn't stand for her to think that. It wasn't true, damn it. Just because he couldn't speak her language . . .

Slowly, he crossed the clearing. He was standing beside her. He hesitated, and then he knelt in front of the grave and bowed his head. It was the only thing he could think of that might get through to her.

At least she'd know that he cared.

It felt funny, being on his knees. It made Harry think back to when he'd been a kid and had to go to church every Sunday. The last time he'd knelt like this had been in church, and it had been one hell of a long time ago— six or seven years, maybe more.

The ground was cold and wet. He could feel it through the knees of his trousers.

Mi hadn't moved. She made no gesture, gave no sign. Her face, pale and streaked with tears, told him nothing.

A hush seemed to have fallen upon the whole world, and in all the universe, the only sound that Harry could distinguish was the dull throb of the blood that pulsed inside his head. It was like being alone in a cathedral.

And Mi . . . she was alone, too.

The backs of his legs were starting to cramp just a little bit. Harry didn't move. Nothing moved. Not even the leaves on the trees. And the war . . . it was someplace else right now.

Mi gasped, and looked up.

"What's the matter? Are you okay?"

Hastily, she scrambled to her feet.

Harry looked. At first, he didn't see anything. Then he did.

It was Ton. He'd come back from wherever he'd disappeared to, and had sneaked up on them without making a sound. How long had he been standing there watching them? One minute? Five?

Harry sighed, and stood up.

Nobody had said anything yet, and nobody had moved. Harry hesitated. He didn't know whether he ought to go away and leave them alone together, or whether he ought to stay here with Mi. He'd do whatever she wanted him to do, he decided.

He glanced at her. She nodded. Did that mean that she wanted him to stay? Probably. Okay then, he'd stay.

Ton said something.

Mi bowed her head.

He repeated it, more loudly this time.

Still, Mi said nothing.

Ton took a step forward. The grave lay between them, raw and new.

Bong sat there, watching everything.

It wasn't right, that they should be fighting like this.

Ton looked at the grave, looked at Mi, and said something else. Mi cried out, and her hand flew up before her face as if to shield it.

"All right. That's enough, now."

Ton ignored him.

"Hey, *that's enough*."

Ton smiled thinly, but his next remark—whatever it meant—brought the blood rushing to Mi's face.

"All right, half-pint. If that's the way it's gotta be . . . but don't say I didn't warn you."

Moving fast, Harry grabbed Ton by the back of his loose shirt and hoisted him off the ground. It was as easy as lifting a puppy. But what could you expect? The kid probably hadn't had a square meal since the day he was born.

"Now, listen to me. Just simmer down and listen to me. I'm fed up with you, understand? Fed up. We're all fed up with you, and we're not going to put up with any more of your crap. We've had enough. So from here on in, you just cool it, huh?"

Ton struggled, all arms and legs, but Harry had him.

He shot a quick look at Mi, just to see how she was taking it. He didn't want to upset her, or offend her, or anything like that. If Mi wanted him to put the kid down . . .

It was okay. Mi was smiling. Well, not exactly smiling, but the corners of her mouth were kind of turned up, and her eyes had a little bit of their sparkle back, and Harry knew that she was with him all the way.

"It's no use trying to get away. I've got you. Now listen to me. Are you going to straighten up, or not?"

Squirming helplessly, Ton hollered something.

"Is that any way to talk to your elders?"

Bong started to giggle. And Mi's eyes were brighter than ever.

Harry grinned, enjoying himself.

Twisting his head up and back—like a damned wild animal, Harry thought later—Ton sank his teeth into Harry's forearm. It hurt like hell. It hurt so bad that without even thinking about it, Harry flung his arm out away from his chest, and Ton went with it, as if he'd been shot out of a sling.

Ton landed on all fours, like a cat. There was a breathless silence.

Harry examined his arm, kneading it with his fingers in an attempt to make it bleed. A puncture wound could be a death warrant in this lousy country. A couple of drops of blood oozed out, bright red. The damn thing would probably be infected by dusk.

Mi started to say something, but Ton shouted her down. And a guy didn't have to be able to speak Viet-namese to understand the gist of what the kid was saying.

Mi and Ton were both talking at once, and neither one of them was paying any attention to Harry.

The kids were worse than the adults, Harry thought darkly. Charlie latched onto them before they could even walk, and taught them how to hate. It was the first thing they learned—how to hate. No wonder they'd been at war for twenty years! Lousy communist bastards. It was enough to make you sick, what they did to little kids.

Ton had finished talking. He was glaring at Mi—waiting for something, Harry thought.

Mi looked at Harry. Then she looked at Ton. And then, as if she'd thought it over and made a decision, she nodded.

Harry wondered what the hell was going on.

Ton turned, and walked away. Was he leaving for good? Going back to Charlie, maybe? Harry noticed that he headed upstream, back the way they'd come.

"Where's he going?"

Mi looked at him expressionlessly.

Bong called out, and Mi shushed her. They talked back and forth for a couple of minutes. It sounded as if Bong was asking questions, and Mi was answering them.

Harry began to feel uneasy. He gazed thoughtfully at Mi. Whose side was she on, anyhow?

"Damn it. Look, I'm sorry. I didn't mean to toss him around. It all kind of got out of hand, you know what I mean?"

Of course she didn't know what he meant. She didn't speak any English, so how the hell *could* she know?

Damned Vietnamese, Harry thought. They ask us to come over here and fight their lousy, stinking war for them . . . the least they could do is to learn how to speak English.

For a while, nobody said a word. They just stood there, looking at one another.

"So what do we do now? Do we all sit around and wait for Ton to come back? Or do we cross the river?"

To his surprise, Mi turned to him and said something. He couldn't understand a word of it, but he had a feeling that it had something to do with the river.

A few hours ago, she'd drawn him a picture of what she wanted to do. If she could draw pictures, she could understand pictures. Dropping to his knees, Harry scraped the grass and leaves away from a square of earth, smoothing it with the palm of his hand so that he could draw upon it. Quickly, using the tip of his forefinger, he sketched the river.

But Mi wasn't watching. She was looking back toward the baby's grave.

"Mi, come on, look at this."

She looked, uncomprehendingly.

"It's the river. That river, over there." He pointed at the river. "And here we are, here's me and you and Bong, and this one's Ton, okay?"

He'd scribbled in little stick-figures, as he spoke.

"Are you with me so far?"

She gave him a shy little smile, and dropped her eyes.

Vietnamese or not, she was a pretty little thing. Plucky, too. He knew grown men who weren't anywhere near as gutsy as Mi seemed to be. You had to admire her, Vietnamese or not.

"Listen to me. We've got to cross the river. The sooner the better, right? Okay then, do we cross here?" He drew his finger across the sketched-in river. "Or do we go farther downstream?"

She seemed to be thinking it over.

Harry waited.

Mi nodded, and drew her own finger across the map.

But what about Bong? We could carry her, Harry thought. But that would hurt. A stretcher would be better. Plenty of bamboo, plenty of vines, why not build a stretcher?

"Here, look at this."

He tried to draw a picture of a stretcher, but he wasn't much of an artist when it came to fancy stuff. Mi studied it for a moment, then gave him a blank look.

"It's a stretcher. Sort of like a bed. You carry people on it. Here, look. See?" He sketched another stick-figure of Bong, lying on the stretcher. "That's Bong. Now do you get it?"

Her face lit up like a Christmas tree, and she said something quick and eager.

Harry set to work. There was plenty of bamboo at the edge of the clearing, more than enough for the eight poles that he figured he'd need. The bamboo made a funny, pulpy sound when he cut into it, not like real wood. But it was good, strong stuff. If they'd had more time, and if Mi had been a little bit stronger, he could have built a raft.

Mi had gone to sit next to Bong. Harry's eyes rested on them for a minute, then moved across the clearing to where the grave was . . . but there wasn't anything he could do about *that,* Harry thought. Better to worry about Mi and Bong and Ton, who were still alive.

He'd finished cutting the poles, and he laid them out on the ground. Two long ones and six shorter ones; the short ones would fit across the long ones and form the bed of the stretcher. So far, so good. Yanking up fistful after fistful of the thick vines that grew along the edge of the river, Harry triple-braided them together and then used them to lash the lengths of bamboo into place.

It would have to be strong. It would have to be strong enough to hold Bong, and strong enough to take a little bit of knocking around in the river. Harry wove more vines back and forth between the bamboo lattice-work of the stretcher, double-knotting everything and tugging at it to make sure that it all held.

"There, that ought to do it."

Mi and Bong watched, fascinated. They'd probably never seen anything like this, Harry thought. He winked at Mi, and she blushed.

What did she really think of him? He'd have given anything to know.

Mi came over, touched it, said something.

"Not bad, is it? You know, it's the first one I've ever made. Honest. I watched a guy make one, but this is the first time I ever tried it by myself."

Mi looked impressed.

"Well, what do you think? Do you think we can manage it?"

She gave him one of those open, big-eyed looks. They'd do fine, Harry thought. Just fine . . . and then he thought of something.

"Do you know how to swim?"

She didn't have a clue.

"Swim. You know—swim. Like this," and he made arm-over-arm swimming motions in the air. "See? Swim. Do you know how to do it?"

Her eyes glued to his, she imitated him.

"Yeah, that's right. But can you do it in the water? In the river? Over there," and he pointed at the river.

Giggling, she nodded.

There was something about the way she laughed . . . he laughed too, because he just couldn't help it. And because he'd done a good job on the stretcher. And because they were finally going to get across the damned river.

Cai Nuoc was over there, on the other side of the river. Cai Nuoc and a hot shower and some decent grub. "Tell you what," he said to Mi, only half-remembering that she couldn't understand. "When we get back to civilization, I'll take you downtown and buy you the biggest, thickest, juiciest steak you ever saw in your whole life, what do you think of that?"

She smiled, hesitantly.

"I'll bet you've never even tasted a steak, have you?"

She didn't know what he was talking about. But it felt good to talk, so he kept talking.

"Well, you'll have one when we get to Cai Nuoc. A big, thick steak smothered in onions. With some french fried potatoes, and maybe a big bowl of coleslaw on the side. Yeah, and a big hunk of chocolate cake for dessert."

Harry stood up. All that talk about food had made him hungry. Mi stood up too.

All they had to do now was to get themselves across the river, and they'd be home free. All of them. The Green Beret types who were running the Cai Nuoc operation were a bunch of smart cookies, and they'd be able to take over. They'd know where Harry's unit was, and they'd know what to do about Mi and Bong . . .

What would they do with Mi, anyhow? It wasn't as if she was a prisoner of war, or anything like that. They'd ask her a couple of questions—Harry'd tell them to take it easy with her—and then they'd turn her loose. But where would she go? How would she eat? Who'd help her take care of Bong?

She'd wanted to go to Saigon. That might not be a bad idea. But what would she do when she got there? She could probably get a job in one of the joints on Tu

Do Street . . . but she wasn't that kind of girl, Harry decided.

Still, she'd have to do something. She had to eat. Maybe she had relatives in Saigon. Yeah, that was probably it. And that was why she'd been so eager to get to Saigon—because she had family there. It all made sense now. Harry felt a lot better knowing that she had relatives in Saigon and that they'd take care of her and Bong. He hated to think of her all alone, on her own.

Maybe he could find out where she was staying. There'd be interpreters in Cai Nuoc. Yeah, and the next time he got an in-country Rest and Recuperation leave, he could go visit her. Wouldn't that be something, visiting with her in Saigon?

Mi was talking to Bong, smiling and pointing at the stretcher. Preparing her, Harry figured. That was a good idea. It'd be a lot easier on everybody, if Bong thought the whole thing was some kind of a game.

Harry carried the stretcher over to where Bong was, and laid it down alongside of her. Mi put her hands under Bong's armpits, and Harry got hold of her legs.

"Easy does it. Look at that! It's a perfect fit!"

Bong looked up at them. She looked scared.

"Hey, tell her it's going to be all right. Tell her that we won't drop her, tell her not to be afraid."

Mi showed Bong how to hold onto the edges of the stretcher. She spoke quietly, and Bong seemed to relax a little bit.

"All ready? Okay then, here we go."

They lifted the stretcher. Even with Bong on it, it hardly weighed anything at all. This was going to be a cinch.

Slowly, testing for sinkholes and bad spots, they waded into the river. At first it was pretty easy going. The current was swift and fairly strong, but there wasn't as much floating debris as there had been yesterday, and the water didn't seem to be quite so deep. They moved forward carefully.

Harry showed Mi how to lower the stretcher a little bit, so that it floated lightly on the surface of the water. Bong cried out in alarm, but Mi reassured her.

"Just like a boat," Harry said. "Nothing to worry about."

It was almost *too* easy.

Out of the corner of his eye, Harry spotted Ton. He was swimming parallel to them, about thirty yards upstream. Following them? Keeping his eye on them? Spotting them for Charlie? Harry didn't know—and he didn't care.

The river bottom fell off steeply then, and Harry almost lost his footing. Bong yelped as the stretcher swayed and the water washed over her legs, and Mi gasped.

"Hold it. Just—just let's hold it right here for a second. Okay?"

The water was a few inches below his armpits. It was up to Mi's neck. And there was no telling how much deeper it would get. They might have to swim for it after all.

Upstream, Ton treaded water and watched.

"Let's see if we can get around it," Harry said. "It might just be a sinkhole."

Moving with the current, they side-stepped downriver. But it didn't get any better. There was a channel, a deep channel, and they were going to have to cross it.

"Come on. We'll take it slow, as slow as we can. Holler if you get into trouble."

A step. Another step. Now the water was up to his

shoulders. He looked back. Bong clung to the sides of the stretcher and stared down at the swirling waters with a look of terror that wrung his heart. Poor, scared little kid.

Mi's chin was under water, but her mouth and nose were still clear. If it just didn't get any deeper . . .

Another step. Harry hesitated. The water level seemed to have stayed the same that time. Maybe they'd gotten through the worst of it. There was only one way to find out.

He took one more step, and now he was sure.

"Come on! We've got it made!"

And then he heard it, and looked up.

B-52 Strato-Fortresses. They were still pretty high up, and he couldn't see them, but he didn't have to see them to know what they were. Mostly, they worked at night. You learned to listen for them. "Puff The Magic Dragon"—that's what the guys called them.

But what the hell were they doing here?

Now Mi heard them. She froze, staring up at the sky. She didn't have to wait very long. Big-bellied and gray, they dropped below the cloud-cover, lower and lower until you could almost read their serial numbers. What did they think they were doing?

"Come on! They can't see us yet. We've got to get to cover!"

Mi didn't move. It was as if she'd been turned to stone.

The first round of charges came slanting down, silent and silvery, a deadly slanting rain of millions and millions and millions of bullets . . . silent, because light traveled faster than sound. The noise would come later. The river bottom surged beneath them, shuddered and settled to stillness. Then, when it was all over, the high-pitched, shrill scream of the shells racked the air.

"Come on! We're sitting ducks, out in the open like this! Come on!"

Damn her! The B-52s circled lazily, getting ready for a second run. What did they think they were doing? Dumping ordnance, maybe. But if they'd been doing that, they wouldn't be circling, they wouldn't be taking aim . . .

The second round rained down, silently, slicing across the surface of the water like so many tiny knives . . . and then afterward, the high-pitched shriek of what had already happened . . .

"Come on! They've got the range now. Move, damn you! *Move!*"

He lunged forward, yanking at the stretcher. Mi stumbled after him.

"That's it. That's the way. We're almost there," Harry told her, trying to coax her along to safety, the way he'd coax a child or an animal. "Just a couple more steps . . ."

They splashed through the shallow water, reached the far bank and scrambled up the slick, muddy slope. The stretcher jolted wildly, and Bong screamed with pain. There wasn't time to be gentle. There wasn't even time to be sorry.

"We've got to take cover. Those bushes—yeah, over there. Don't worry about Bong. I've got her." He scooped her up off the stretcher, and she screamed again. "She's all right, she's all right. Come on! Here, back under these bushes. Yeah, that's right. Lie down. Like that. Yeah. Okay, here's Bong. Keep her quiet, and keep your head down, like this. Watch me. Yeah, that's right."

He could hear the drone of the big engines, throbbing louder and louder as the Dragon Ships dropped down for another run. Three runs over the same damned place. In broad daylight, too. This wasn't any ordnance drop. Those babies were after something—but what?

Mi huddled next to him, her eyes shut. She looked as if she expected to die. Maybe she was right.

Someone was shouting. Harry frowned, and thought maybe he was imagining things. Then he remembered that Ton had been in the river, and that Ton might still be in the river, and realized that it was Ton who was shouting.

Shouting. Why? Was he hurt? Calling for help?

"What's the matter with him? Does he need help? Was he hit?"

Mi's face was blank, terrified.

Harry stood up. He saw Ton and blinked, and looked again. It was unbelievable. It was like a World War II movie, in technicolor. Ton was standing there in the shallow water, shaking his fist at the airplanes and yelling his head off. Like a goddam Jap at Okinawa, Harry thought.

"Get your head down! Hit the dirt, you stupid son of a bitch!"

Way up in the sky, the squadron of B-52s banked lazily. They were so far away that they didn't even look like real airplanes. Then they straightened out, got their bearings, and dove.

Harry ran toward Ton. He didn't think about it. He just did it.

"They'll kill all of us, you stupid bastard! *All of us!*"

Ton had stopped shouting. He stood very still, not seeming to notice the airplanes, or Harry either. Had he been hit? Was he in shock? What the hell had happened to him?

Slowly, Ton turned his head and looked at Harry. His

face was calm, almost religious. Except for his eyes, which were open but expressionless, he might have been asleep. Or dead.

"Come on!"

To the left, little fountains of gray water spurted up and stitched themselves silently across the surface of the river. Harry watched, fascinated. It was almost as if the shells were living creatures, deadly little animals with eyes and ears and noses . . . deadly, hunting animals, like the big German shepherds they used at Dak To.

Mi screamed.

*Haa-lee.* That's what she called him. *Haa-lee.*

The shrill whine of the ordnance reverberated through the air, filling his ears and bounding through his brain like an electric shock. Harry wanted to yell back at it, to drown it out with the sound of his own, human voice.

*By the time you can hear it, it's all over.*

They hadn't been hit, then. Because they could still hear. They were still alive.

Then a new line of shells came down—Harry couldn't hear them, but he could see them hitting the ground and sending up little geysers of mud as they made their way toward the place where he stood—and before he could move or even think about moving, the world exploded and a pit of darkness yawned at his feet and Harry thought, So this is what it's like to die.

# EIGHT

He lay where he'd fallen, the upper part of his body in the mud of the river bank, his legs dangling in the shallow water. Being careful to remain expressionless (for Ton must not guess at what she was feeling) Mi bent over Haa-lee, and gently wiped the mud from his eyes and mouth. He was unconscious, but he was breathing.

Behind her—far, far away, it seemed to Mi—Bong had started to cry.

"Go and see what's wrong with her," Mi told Ton.

Wordlessly, he went.

Alone, Mi gazed down upon Haa-lee's motionless body.

All of this was Ton's fault. All of it. They might have been safe, if it hadn't been for Ton. *Come on!* Ton had shouted at the airplanes. *There's a Yankee down here, a*

*big, ugly, round-eyed Yankee! Come and kill him for us!*
*Come and kill the Yankee!*

And Haa-lee had rushed out, rushed from the safety
of the thicket into the river, into the deadly rain of
bullets . . .

Feeling giddy and sick to her stomach, Mi sat down
upon a flat rock and pressed her hands to her aching
head. She was trembling all over. A tiny pulse pounded
at the base of her throat, and a cold perspiration
drenched her body.

Oh, Haa-lee!

She looked up. The sky was empty now. Empty and
white and hot. It was going to rain. Mi's eyes moved
wearily from the sky to the trees to the swollen river and
then to the far bank, to the place where Little Brother
slept. Searching through the patches of light and leaf and
shadow, Mi sought the mound of freshly turned earth
that marked the grave. Had any of the bullets hit it? She
shuddered, and looked away.

Now there was Haa-lee. So still. Scarcely breathing.
Must he die, too?

Footsteps. It was Ton. He stood there before her, arms
akimbo, thinking . . . what?

"Well? What now?"

Slowly, Mi shook her head.

"Is he dead?" asked Ton.

"No."

"He looks dead."

"Well, he's not."

Ton squatted down and peered at Haa-lee with un-
disguised curiosity. He stared and stared without saying a word, and finally his silence grated on Mi's nerves.

"What are you looking at?"

"His face. He's got little hairs all over it, thousands of

them. Like a monkey! Are their women hairy, too?"

"How should I know? And what difference does it make?" Abruptly, Mi got to her feet. "We've got to go for help!"

"Help?" Ton was incredulous. "For an American soldier? You know as well as I do what happens to people who help American soldiers."

Mi looked at Haa-lee. So helpless. So still. His life was in her hands. Just as Little Brother's life had been in her hands . . .

"He's hurt badly. *Someone* will help. We can't just let him die."

But Ton shook his head. "Not here. Not in this province. People are afraid."

This was true. Too much had happened, too many had died.

"But Haa-lee is different!"

"To *you*, perhaps."

There was a silence, an uneasy silence.

Ton shifted his weight from one foot to the other, and gazed contemplatively into the jungle, toward Cai Nuoc. "We were going to go to Saigon. We were going to find Papa, don't you remember?"

Yes, she remembered.

Hidden in the sheltering green of the bamboo, Bong was crying again. Hopelessly, as if she knew that no one would come to comfort her, no matter how much she cried.

"Her leg hurts," said Ton, "and she's hungry. If we could get to Cai Nuoc . . ."

"Oh, leave me alone!"

Surprised, Ton stared at her.

"Stop jabbering. Let me think."

A strange, brooding stillness had crept over the jungle.

The air was thick with moisture, suffocating with heat. Above their heads, the rain-heavy clouds piled one on top of the other and the sky darkened to a yellowish gray. Now and then a bird winged silently past, seeking cover.

The storm was very close. A tongue of lightning flickered on the horizon, traced a jagged white path across the sky, vanished.

"We've got to move him," Mi said suddenly.

Ton gave her a strange, guarded look. "Move him?"

"Yes! Look at the river! Look how high the water is. If there's a flash flood, he'll be swept away!"

Ton neither moved nor spoke.

"You'll have to help me."

"No."

"But I can't move him by myself!"

"Then leave him where he is."

"Ton! Please help me. *Please!*"

He looked around, as sharply as if she'd slapped him. He looked . . . frightened.

"You'd let him die?" Mi asked quickly, pressing her advantage. "You'd leave him here to drown? Even after he tried to save your life?"

Ton scowled. "What are you talking about? He's never done anything for me."

"But he has! Just now. That's why he ran back to the river, don't you see? He was safe. All three of us were safe. But when he saw you standing out in the open like that, he thought you'd gone crazy. He was trying to rescue you."

"Do you think I'm stupid?" demanded Ton. "You know as well as I do that he wasn't trying to save my life. He could hear what I was saying, couldn't he?"

"He could hear you, yes. But he couldn't understand you. He doesn't speak Vietnamese."

Above their heads, the black clouds gathered and thunder rumbled. The surface of the river had become as smooth as glass, grayish glass. There wasn't much time, and yet she did not dare to hurry Ton, lest she force him into a determined refusal.

He was looking at Haa-lee now, strangely. Mi watched him and wondered what was in his heart. Hatred? Compassion? Indifference? Perhaps . . . pity?

"It doesn't make any difference whether we move him or not. He'll probably die, no matter what we do."

Mi waited, quietly.

"All right then. What do you want me to do?"

"Here," said Mi. "I'll take his shoulders, and you take his legs. Both of them. That's right. Have you got him?" Mi tucked her own hands firmly beneath Haa-lee's armpits, and braced herself. "All right, now lift!"

Haa-lee didn't budge.

"Ooof! He's heavy!"

"Let's try it again. One . . . two . . . *three!*"

But it was no use.

"He's too heavy for us!" said Ton. "It would take two men and a bullock to move him. Let's just leave him where he is. He'll be all right."

"No!"

Ton gave her a flat, indifferent look.

"I won't leave him here to die! I won't!"

"Well, maybe we could drag him."

Mi frowned. Hurt as badly as Haa-lee seemed to be, it might kill him to be dragged up the uneven slope of the bank. Perhaps Ton was right. Perhaps they would do best to simply leave him here. Yet if the river flooded . . .

"Make up your mind." Ton let Haa-lee's lifeless legs drop back into the mud. "Either we drag him, or we leave him."

It was starting to rain. The jungle was dark, its colors muted and tinged with gray. The wind began to rise, rustling through the tall grasses, clacking the palm fronds one against the other and making the bamboo sway before it.

"We've *got* to move him!"

They propped Haa-lee up between them, his head drooping forward onto his chest and his legs dragging lifelessly behind him. Mi and Ton each took one of Haa-lee's arms, huge and limp, and draped it over their shoulders.

"All right, let's go."

It was raining harder now. Mi's hair lay flat against her head like a helmet, and her shirt and trousers, already soaked through, clung immodestly to her body. The wind swept across the river in ever-stronger gusts, flattening the tall grasses and driving the rain before it in slanting, gray sheets.

The river itself had become choppy and turbulent, stung to anger by the wind and the pelting rain. Its churning waters plucked feverishly at the crumbling bank, tearing away whole chunks of the raw, red earth and swirling them into its depths. Even now, the place where Haa-lee had been lying was covered with a film of deepening water.

"It's going to flood."

"I knew it would. I knew it!"

"Well, come on. Let's get out of here."

Slipping and sliding, they started up the slope. It was slow, breathless work. Haa-lee hung between them like a wet sack of meal, and his enormous weight tugged them continually backward, so that it was all they could do to keep from being pulled back down the mud-slicked bank and into the river.

Another step. Another. Lightning arched vividly across the rain-blackened sky, and the thunder crashed about their heads as if the heavens themselves would topple.

"It's no good! He's too heavy!"

"But we're almost there!" pleaded Mi.

Her arms were beginning to ache, and her shoulder, where she bore most of Haa-lee's weight, was numb. She stubbed her toe on a rock and gasped with pain.

"What's wrong?"

"Nothing. It's nothing. I'm all right. Come on!"

"Look at the river!"

"Never mind. Come on. Hurry!"

The ground wasn't as steep here as it had been at the river's edge, but all of the grass had been burned away —a fire, perhaps?—and the mud was ankle-deep. It sucked at Mi's feet like quicksand, cold and slimy. The rain poured down as if from a bucket, and it was difficult to see more than an arm's length ahead. The wind had shifted, too. It blew hard in their faces, pushing them back like a gigantic, invisible hand pressed at their chests.

"How much farther?" shouted Ton.

"Just to the top of the rise! Just a few more steps!"

Suddenly, her legs flew out from under her and she felt herself slipping backward. She clutched wildly at Haa-lee's arm, but her fingers closed on air . . . and then, mud. Before she could do more than pull herself to a sitting position, it was too late. Haa-lee's body had collapsed into a loose welter of flopping arms and legs, and pitched back down the slope.

"I couldn't help it. I couldn't hold him by myself. He was too heavy."

Mi said nothing. Haa-lee lay about halfway down the slope, motionless, his descent checked by a jagged outcropping of gray rock. He was very still, so still that Mi wondered if he was alive or dead. The rain had washed the mud from his face. His eyes were closed.

Oh, Haa-lee!

"He'll be all right," Ton said. "The water won't come up as far as that. Not unless there's a flood. We can come back for him when it stops raining."

"But we can't leave him like this."

Ton turned, and ran toward the semi-shelter of the bamboo thicket. Just before he disappeared into the swaying green of the jungle, he stopped and shouted something at Mi, but his words were lost in the howling of the wind.

Alone, Mi got slowly to her feet. She started back down the slope toward Haa-lee. But it was no good. Without Ton, she could do nothing for him. Nothing. She stopped, and pushed her wet hair back away from her face.

All about her, the storm screamed its fury.

It can't go on like this for very long, Mi thought. And as soon as it stops, we can come back . . .

With a last look at Haa-lee, Mi turned and trudged back up the hill, toward the bamboo. The wind had changed direction yet again, and now it was at her back.

Well, she'd tried. She'd done her best. Even Ton had tried . . .

She was crying, and her tears mingled with the rain that poured down her face.

.     .     .

The storm lasted for several hours.

For a while, Ton amused Bong by telling her stories —legends of ancient Annam, tales of the Jade Emperor and his Celestial Court, and other stories—stories of recklessly brave men and women who fought against the Japanese and then against the French, stories that Mi had never heard before. Hung Ba's stories, Mi thought. But she said nothing.

Worn out with fear and fatigue, and lulled by the sound of the pattering rain, Bong rested her head against Ton's shoulder, closed her eyes, and was soon asleep.

The thicket that sheltered them was of bamboo inter-mixed with banana trees, and the intricate weave of the two kinds of leaves—the banana huge and flat, with the slender bamboo filling in the chinks—afforded a shelter that was nearly as good as a hut. Water dripped through in several places, but not enough to be worrisome. Out-side, the wind wailed forlornly about them, but the lashing rain had given way to a slow, steady drizzle.

Mi shivered, and wished that they had a fire.

She looked at Ton. His eyes were blank and distant, and she could not even guess at his thoughts.

"It's not raining much now. I could go and get Haa-lee."

Ton looked up. "What would you do with him? There's barely enough room in here for the three of us. Where would we put him?"

They spoke in whispers, so as not to awaken Bong.

"Perhaps he's conscious. In pain."

"What if he is? *We* can't do anything for him."

"But he'll wonder where we've gone."

Ton shrugged, and said nothing.

The thought of Haa-lee—hurt and helpless, lying

there in the mud and thinking that they'd left him to die—wrung Mi's heart. She could not bear to think of him like that.

"Where are you going?" asked Ton.

"To see if he's all right."

Mi crept out of the thicket and stood up. Everything was gray—the sky, the rain, the river—everything. Haa-lee lay where they'd left him, on his back. He hadn't moved, and his eyes were still closed. Mi splashed quickly through the mud until she was beside him. Hesitantly, she touched his arm. He was cold, so cold that for a moment she thought he was dead. But when she slipped her hand into his shirt and laid it against his chest, she could feel the slow, strong pulsing of his heart.

The rain had become a fine, drizzling mist. It might stop soon, or it might last all night.

There was nothing she could do for Haa-lee. It was enough that he was alive. She left him, and returned to the relative shelter of the thicket.

"Is he still there?"

Mi nodded.

"And is he still alive?"

Again she nodded.

Nothing else was said for a long, long time.

When the rain finally stopped, it was too late to think of travel. The sun set in a glorious burst of color, and darkness fell like a shroud. Another day was gone. Little Brother was dead. And Saigon seemed farther than the moon.

Mi's wet clothes clung uncomfortably to her skin, and Ton's teeth were chattering. Searching through Haa-lee's pockets, Mi found the last of the matches. They were soaked and muddy, useless. After several attempts to make them flame, she threw them into the river.

128

She was cold and hungry. Ton went to look for some bananas, but it was too dark. He came back empty-handed and irritable. If only we had some rice, Mi thought wistfully. Or some tea. It seemed such a long time since they'd had rice or tea.

Mercifully, Bong was still asleep.

Now there was nothing to do but wait for morning. Ton crept back into the shelter, curled himself into a ball and closed his eyes. He lay very still. Mi did not know whether he was asleep or not, but her own stomach cramped with hunger, and made sleep impossible.

Carefully, she groped her way to the place where Haa-lee lay. She sat down beside him, cross-legged, hugging herself for warmth. After a time, she reached out and felt his forehead. It was cool. He had no fever, then.

She sighed, and stared into the darkness.

Tomorrow . . . what would happen tomorrow? They couldn't stay here. The rising waters would drive them to higher ground in a day or two. And what would become of Haa-lee?

We can't move him, Mi thought sadly. He's too heavy. Must we leave him here to die?

Why had he done it? Why had he run out into the river? To save Ton's life? It didn't make sense.

Again, her fingers stroked Haa-lee's forehead.

"What are you doing? Is he dead?"

"I thought you were asleep."

"But what are you doing?"

"Nothing. Just sitting here and . . ."

"And what?"

"Thinking."

"Thinking about him?" demanded Ton.

"Thinking about all of us. Thinking about what we're going to do tomorrow."

"What *are* we going to do?"

"You'll have to go to Cai Nuoc, and get help."

"We don't need help. We can manage Bong by ourselves."

"Haa-lee needs help."

It was easier to speak of these things in the dark. Much, much easier. Mi wondered why that should be.

"Even if I went, who'd help an American?"

"Other Americans," Mi said quietly.

"But . . ."

"I've been thinking about it," said Mi. "Cai Nuoc is a big place, full of Catholics. There must be some Americans there, too. The Catholics always like to have Americans near, to protect them. You told me so yourself! Now, here's my plan. Bong and I will hide someplace, near enough to see what happens but far enough away so that they won't be able to see us. Then . . ."

"*Who* won't be able to see you?" interrupted Ton.

"The Americans. The ones who come for Haa-lee."

"And how will they know where to find him?"

"You're going to tell them. You're going to leave a message at the church. All you have to do is tell someone that there's a wounded American soldier lying by the river just across from Vinh Luc. You can do that much, can't you?"

"Suppose I leave my message with the wrong people?"

"You won't."

"Why won't I?"

"He was trying to save your life."

There was a silence.

"He was stupid!"

Mi said nothing. Ton must be allowed to think this through by himself.

"He may be dead before morning," said Ton.

130

That was true, too.

"It would be better for everyone if he died."

"Not for him," said Mi.

Another silence. Would Ton go for help? And even if he agreed to go, could she trust him? Or would he betray Haa-lee to men who would come here and kill him? Ton was silent for so long that Mi thought he might have gone to sleep. She leaned back, and closed her eyes. She ached with hunger and weariness, but her thoughts whirled round and round inside her head and would not let her rest.

"Mi, do you think we'll find Papa?"

"Of course I do."

"But Saigon is so big, and there are so many people like us . . ."

"Like us? What do you mean?"

"Refugees," said Ton.

"Don't worry, we'll find Papa. We know where he is. He's at Bien Hoa."

"Do you think he knows about the village?"

"Perhaps."

"Well, suppose he's on his way back here? Suppose he's already left Bien Hoa?"

"He hasn't," said Mi. "Go to sleep."

Ton stood up, stretched, and went back to the thicket to sleep.

Mi stayed where she was, with Haa-lee. In case he wakes up, she thought. In case he needs me.

The hours passed, and Haa-lee did not stir. The stars came out, and transformed the velvety sky into a sort of clock. Now Mi could measure the long hours against the slow movement of the stars. Was she asleep? Was she awake? Was it possible to be both asleep and awake at the same time?

She must have slept, because when she opened her eyes the stars were gone and the first rose colors of dawn had already begun to streak the eastern sky.

Haa-lee lay beside her. He had not moved. His eyes were still closed. She touched his forehead . . . and then she was awake, completely awake, bending over Haa-lee, holding his cold, stiff head between her two hands, not believing that this could happen, that Haa-lee could die.

Ah! Haa-lee!

She sat back on her heels, and stared at him. Dead. Haa-lee was dead.

Yet she could not bring herself to believe it. Again she reached out her hand, touched him. Perhaps . . . no. He was dead. His flesh was cold. Stiff. He had died during the night, while she slept.

If only she hadn't slept . . .

And then, the airplanes came back.

She watched them, dazed. At first, she thought it was a dream. There were a lot of airplanes, many more than there had been yesterday. She tried to count them, and could not. They droned above her, a dull silver color against the pale, white dawn.

It was not a dream.

So, we will die. All of us. In a few moments, we will be with Mama . . .

The first bombs dropped from the bellies of the airplanes. Strange bombs! Big and white and billowing, like huge mushrooms made of white cloth. They fell slowly, so slowly. They floated down, white in the white sky. Now Mi could see that there were tiny black objects dangling from the mushrooms, swinging back and forth, back and forth . . .

Mi looked, rubbed her eyes and looked again. The

things that were attached to the billowing white canopies, the things that hung at the ends of the strings
and swayed back and forth—they were men!

Dozens of them. Hundreds of them. But how could
such things be?

"Ton! *Ton!* Come here!"

He emerged from the thicket sleepily.

"Look!" She pointed. "Up there! Do . . . do you see
them?"

"But—they're men!"

They stood side by side, staring up at the sky.

"It's an invasion!" exclaimed Ton. "Paratroopers.
We've got to get out of here!"

The first of the men had landed now. Fascinated, Mi
watched as they fell, one by one, soundlessly down
through the trees and the tangled undergrowth, their
white parasols collapsing silently over their heads. She
tried to count them, and couldn't. There were too many.
It would be foolish to run away, she decided. It would be
best if they remained right here, with Haa-lee. Surely,
when the Americans found them here with Haa-lee,
they'd understand . . .

Off to the right, a machine-gun spattered bullets into
the jungle.

Bong woke up, and called for Mi.

"Go to her!" Mi told Ton. "Tell her to be still! You
stay there with her, and I'll stay here, with Haa-lee."

"But they'll kill us!"

"No they won't."

Another burst of gun-fire shattered the early-morning
stillness. And another.

"We ought to make a run for it . . ."

"No! Listen to them!" whispered Mi. "They're frightened, and they're shooting at everything that moves! Don't you remember what Haa-lee was like, how frightened he was?"

Ton hesitated.

"Go to Bong! Do as I say!"

Across the river, there was a *bang!* a quick orange flame, and then billowing, inky black smoke.

Bong screamed.

"Go to her! Keep her still!"

"Mi, look! Over there!"

There were three of them, three American soldiers. They wore the same green-and-brown dappled clothing as Haa-lee wore, and each of them was carrying a machine-gun.

"Don't move," whispered Mi. "They've already seen us. Don't do anything that might make them shoot us."

"They'll shoot us no matter what we do! We ought to try and run for it!"

"No. If we run, they'll think we killed Haa-lee."

"Killed . . . is he dead?"

"Yes," said Mi. "He's dead."

Ton looked at her. "If *he's* dead, then so are we. They'll kill us for sure!"

"Hush!"

The soldiers came slowly toward them, their guns aimed and ready to fire. They hadn't seen Haa-lee yet. But they couldn't possibly think that we killed Haa-lee . . .

"Mi! Mi! Where are you?"

Bong! One of the soldiers whirled about and leveled his gun at the thicket, and Ton lunged at him. The soldier lost his footing and staggered backward, dropping his gun in the mud. But one of the other soldiers— a tall, beefy-looking man—lifted his gun and brought it down on Ton's head, hard. It made a dull, thunking sound, and Ton crumpled silently to the ground.

On his feet again, the first soldier aimed his machine-gun into the thicket.

"No! Don't shoot! It's only my sister, only a little girl . . ."

But the bullets leaped from the barrel of his gun, shredding through the bamboo as if it were made of paper . . . and Mi did not hear Bong cry out again.

"Murderers! Killers! They were only children . . . *children!*"

The tall soldier slapped her, so hard that she stumbled and almost fell. Her ears rang, and tears leaped to her eyes.

"Go ahead! Kill me! I don't care!"

He hit her again, and this time she fell to her knees. He pointed his gun at her, and said something. Fool! Did he think that she was afraid of him?

She leaped at him, her fingers clawing wildly at the soft flesh of his face and eyes. He pushed her away, holding her at arm's length.

"Murderer!"

He flung her to the ground. Crouching there, she saw the fire leap from the muzzle of his gun.

The universe itself seemed to open beneath her in a flaming burst of sound and crimson that was beyond pain, beyond everything . . . and then there was nothing, and she knew no more.

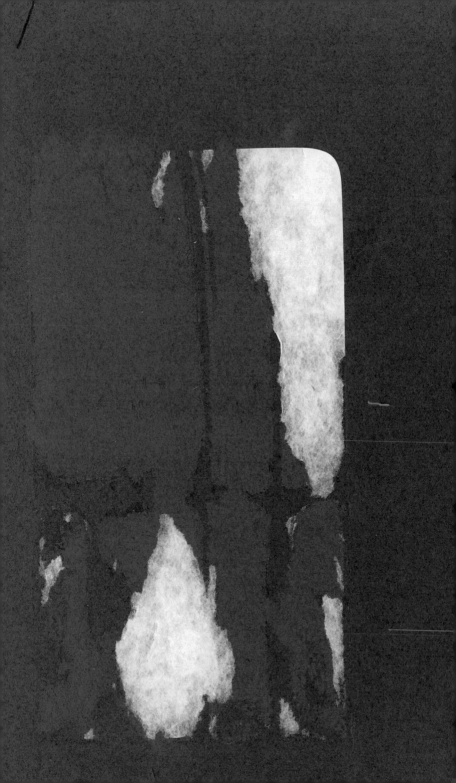